Gracie Emerson

The creek was our oasis. One by one we followed the simply etched path through the woods to the place where the field opened up. As we made our way across the enchanted landscape, beautiful words entreated my mind. They spoke of a creek, wild and free.

The water traveling over stones, year after year, created an erosion of hearts. For me, it had been sixteen years, of a lifetime etched by waters. Yes, there were sounds, but the echoes of silence were most endearing and so complete. The creek, had so many stories to tell.

The intricate patterns of the rocks glistened in the light of the sun, as I turned them in my hands to examine what made each one unique. Mama always said, "God is an artist." I understood what she meant about how, "everything in nature is a perfect interpretation of itself, just as God designed. A beauty that can never be captured on canvas, but is painted only on the heart."

Elizabeth ran up behind me and clutched my shoulders, as I leaned over the creek to study the shadows and rhythmic movements of the water making its way downstream. She was the youngest of us girls, five years old, and full of life. "Gracie," she asked, " How far is it to Heaven?" I was the oldest and helped Mama with the children. Little Eliza, I called her, had captured my heart. Her hazel eyes spoke of something ethereal. She was truly curiosity's child. In my mind's eye, she looked like an angel. Her name, like all of our names, was a family name.

Not knowing much about Heaven myself, I softly replied, "Eliza, Heaven is just beyond the stars." Smiling, she reached her eyes up to the sky, as if she were satisfied.

Hettie May came running down the hill carrying a hopeful grin. She was the next oldest sister to me. Almost breathless as she dropped to the ground, she told us Papa had just come in from town with a surprise for us girls. Curiously, I inquired, "Hettie May, do tell! Do tell!" "I don't know, Gracie. Let's go see," she said smiling. We all made our way back up the hill to the wooden fence and climbed over one after another. Running quickly out of the thicket, we could see the house and a glimmer of Papa on the front porch rocker. His smile growing wider as we approached him.

"Hello Ladies," he said expectantly. "How are my beauties doing today?" In unison, we all chanted "fine" as we tilted our heads to the side in some beauty like fashion. Papa knew all the right words to say to make us feel special.

Fresh aromas of tea brewing and bread rising emanated all about the house as we tentatively made our entrance. Mama was a wonderful hostess, and her beauty only enhanced her hospitality.

After enjoying our tea accompanied by fresh, jam covered bread, Papa directed us outside to his wagon for the great, great unveiling. Overwhelmed with excitement, we all took our places around the wagon and waited in anticipation. "Everyone, close your eyes now," instructed Papa, as he reached into the wagon, and pulled out an apple crate that sounded full with joy. "Papa!" I said. "Did you really? Did you Papa? You got us a kitten?" We all danced around the wagon in a sort of conniption dance, singing, "kitten, kitten, we got a kitten, kitten, kitten, we got a kitten." Papa laughed, and his dimples sparkled like diamonds as if his highest calling was to share happiness with his girls. "Girls," he said, "don't you want to lay your eyes on the little creature before you celebrate it so?" Laughing as we watched his every move, the apple crate opened. Peering over the top was the most adorable amber colored kitten we had ever seen. The eyes shone like starlights, and her paws were a dancer's delight. Fur soft and shiny and a temperament sweet and curious, we each took our turn holding her, and by evening decided to name her Amber, inspired by her beautiful coat of fur. After dark, Papa made his way outside to head back home. Hugging his neck graciously, we each said our goodbyes.

Papa had only ever loved one woman—one beautiful woman. Elizabeth Pearl Emerson moved through the world like an angel on earth, with her light, graceful steps; peace ebbed and flowed from her countenance. Most called her a natural beauty – I called her Pippa Pearl. To me, she was a treasure from the sea; the rarest of pearls, with skin that glowed as the light shone on her finely bred bones. Her eyes alight with hues of iridescent green, softly painted in flecks of yellow and blue, and pupils that opened and closed with the sun's kiss. When Pippa Pearl looked at me, I knew all was well with the world, and somehow, I knew somebody loved me – loved me, unconditionally. In her eyes, the possibilities were endless. I thought God put her on earth to believe in people. After all, He loves us through His creations, and Pippa Pearl was truly—one of His finest creations. Overflowing with love and passion for everything good and true, Pippa Pearl painted her love on my heart.

The spring air was fresh and fragrant. Petals decorated the home place, while birds serenaded in tones of heavenly welcome chimes. Tears ran down my cheeks as I rocked little Eliza in my arms. Papa said a prayer as Pippa Pearl made her final earthly resting place. I wanted to say something poetic, something of the memories I held in my heart, but the wound was too fresh, too open. All I could do was clutch to something I loved, something that was dear to me. In that moment, I understood that little Eliza might be the beneficiary of the love bestowed upon me by Pippa Pearl. She was gifted with those ethereal eyes, that curious heart and that hopeful spirit. It would be my honor, my privilege, to share all I knew of her Grandmother, Elizabeth Pearl Emerson. I was no poet, nor a writer, but that night I began capturing memories on paper, to share with Eliza and the rest.

I wept into my pillow as I remembered what Pippa Pearl had said to me, "Gracie, never forget who you are — that you are beautiful and dearly loved." In her eyes, I was someone. Someone unique. Even as I moved through the world awkwardly and a bit afraid; she gave me confidence. She gave me grace. Over the months and years after her passing, I uncovered little things of her life that gave mine more meaning. Little eccentricities of every kind and passion, unfolding who my Grandmother truly was. She was of rare beauty and of rare heart. Her kindness gave me hope in humanity. Her faith gave me hope in Heaven. Her love of all things beautiful gave me a different view of the world, and all that belonged to it. As I discovered more of who she was, I began to capture her essence into my own heart. She knew that love was a catalyst for hope. She believed in the unbelievable.

A year had passed since we said our goodbyes to Pippa Pearl. The illusions of spring captivated the farm, and new life began to blossom. It seemed that spring always came to remind us that after death comes new life.

Humming hopeful melodies, my sisters and I were tending to our chores, as we welcomed another day. Mama had purchased beautiful new fabrics in town to fashion our spring dresses. As noon approached she stepped outside holding the most alluring dress I had ever seen. "Gracie," she said. "Come try on your new dress love. Let's make sure it's a perfect fit." I leaped up the stairs and followed Mama inside. She led me beside her sewing machine. I slipped the dress over my head and smoothed it down over my body. It fit like a glove.

A girl blooming into a woman — I felt like a spring blossom. The fabric was a little silkier than usual, in colors only springtime could produce. Florals danced all over, as the soft pastel hues shimmered in the light.

Before I made my way outside to show off my new attire, I stopped in front of the mirror and pulled my hair up into a loose bun. Mama's lip color was on the vanity. I smeared just enough on my lips to highlight their fullness. I grinned as I caught my reflection posing in the mirror, and then made my way outside.

"Introducing Gracie Emerson," I announced. The girls were elated. "You look like a princess," Hettie Mae exclaimed. "A true beauty," said Ginny. Eliza and Evelyn ran up to me with mouths open wide in awe and began to caress the dress. I had never felt prettier. The girls' hearts were overjoyed for me, and they knew Mama was creating a thing of beauty for them too.

Mama looked on smiling from the front porch rocker at

all the commotion. She knew she had done well. Her fabric was stunning, and her pattern was flattering. Mama took pride in how we presented ourselves, and it always showed in her craftsmanship.

We practiced our promenade around the yard before time to get back to chores. I never wanted to take my new dress off, but Sunday church was in a few days, and I could debut it there. As we made our way around, I saw dust rising up the road that led down to the house. From a distance, my eyes could not make out the traveler. As he slowly approached on horseback, a most handsome face came into view.

The girls and I became silent, not sure whether to look and welcome him in or appear not to notice. I decided to not notice and got busy about my chores, acting as if I performed them in beautiful dresses and lipstick and such. Tossing my head about to add a hint of mystery, I glanced over my shoulder to see the other girls all in a row staring down the drive ever so obviously. "Have a little dignity," I thought to myself. But, after all, I was the oldest and the wisest and had read at least part of one Shakespearean romance. He finished his poetic entrance, followed by a most entrancing dismount. Then he tied his horse to the gate. I continued to be busy, so to not look anxious about his arrival.

"Good afternoon," he recited to the girls, as they looked on curiously. One by one they chanted "Good afternoon" — everyone but me. I was too enthralled in my work, to notice. Besides, I knew from my readings that he might need to come closer for a proper greeting. Trying hard not to look to the right, nor to the left, I saw in my peripheral view a pair of leather riding boots coming towards me; trodding a path over the soft green grass.

"And how are you my lady," I heard from the right side. Turning my head slowly, while hoping that the words would find me, I said, "Well, and you?" With a timid grin and illustrious eyes, he said, "Much better now, thank you for asking." I could not hide the smile beneath my nose any longer, so I tried no more. Nodding in agreement, I inhaled deeply to gain my composer.

In a moment, as I looked directly into his eyes, I was swept away, like time ceased to exist. A light emanated between us. Walter Lee was the most admired bachelor in town. The towns' people called him Walt for short. Tall, dark and handsome was an understatement. Chestnut brown curls and blue eyes to contrast; I could not imagine what brought him to our farm. He might have come to talk to Papa about doing some work, or possibly about church business—but with me, he lingered.

After a bit of small talk, Walter interrupted, "Gracie, I had hoped to have the opportunity to make your acquaintance sooner, but as fate unfolds, I'll be leaving tomorrow to serve my duty for our country. Before I leave, I wanted to let you know how I feel. My heart holds a special place for you Gracie, and it always has. I would be honored if you would allow me to write to you while I'm away."

I reached deep down into my soul and tried to remember what Pippa Pearl had said to me about not forgetting who I was, and as I looked that handsome man in the eyes, the words "It will be my pleasure," were all I could produce.

His eyes smiled as he spoke, "Thank you, Gracie. When I return, perhaps we shall dance." "Perhaps we shall," I whispered.

As the fall leaves made their descent and the air became ripe with coolness, the farm took on an autumn glow. Spring and autumn were always my favorites. There was something about the new life of spring and the falling away of autumn that touched my heart. It was in those times that I remembered Pippa Pearl the most.

On Saturdays, Daddy would take a trip into town to purchase supplies for the farm and other necessities. If my chores were done well, he would bring me along.

Beginning our journey before the sun peeked over the horizon, I loved to watch the dawn of day over the countryside. Traveling, I imagined my spirit soaring on wings—a creature freed from captivity. There was something about leaving the familiar to discover the fresh and unknown that illuminated everything within me. Interesting silhouettes, aromas and harmonious vibrations of voices, beautifully culminating in unison; it was all so enticing to me.

We pulled up to Wilson's General Store, and Daddy tied off the wagon. He always started his morning with a cup of coffee and a visit with his childhood ally, Mr. Jake Wilson. "Well, look what the cat drug in," Mr. Wilson chuckled out his usual greeting. "I see my friend John and his beautiful daughter have come in to visit some city folks."

Mr. Wilson and his wife Lucille lived above the store and kept busy about its business. After exchanging pleasantries, I would meander curiously down the Main Street of town and leave Daddy to his dealings.

There was a gentle breeze blowing softly against my face. The towns' air was different than on the farm, it seemed. As I inhaled it, the daydreams flourished in dancing motions in my mind. The dance I envisioned most was the one with Walter Lee. My heart rising to the surface as the breeze gently ran its way through my hair. "Perhaps we shall," I reminisced. The vision he painted on my eyes that spring day had affected me — all the way down to my soul.

Raising my eyes upward for an orientation of place; so lost in thought, I had wandered to the end of Main Street. Reality arrived as I peered into the barbershop window.

The men waved hello, and I gestured back with an out of place smile. I gazed down the street to take notice of all the activity, the hustle and bustle of people coming and going. Something about this place energized me. Something about it brought together another piece of the puzzle of who I was.

"Gracie Emerson," I heard a voice call from the dressmaker's shop. I cautiously stepped towards the door and peeped in. There was a handsome man, and I assumed his wife, standing behind a beautiful wooden counter. Luscious fabrics lined shelves like a Parisian Village. The colors pure and bright, dyed on the finest patterned cloth.

Her hair was golden blonde with a hint of curl. Pulled back into a hand carved silver clip, loosely and elegantly. The dress was fine and feminine, in blue satin. My cousin, Olivia Emory, stood in that dress shop like a Montgomery Ward catalog model.

Her family's farm was adjacent to ours. Her mother and mine were sisters. Aunt Sophie was three years older than Mama, and every bit as beautiful and kind. Olivia and I were born in the same year. I was a spring baby, and she was a winter. Like the winter tends to be icy, so was Olivia. Beauty was innate to her; with eyes like crystal pools of aquamarine, and the most beautiful complexion you had ever seen.

With her snide remarks and conceded stance, I often wished we weren't even kin. I knew about beauty. Pippa Pearl was a different kind of beauty. She wore kindness as her crown.

Olivia's presence loomed large over the shop as she turned haughtily in front of the mirror waiting for praises from the proprietor and his wife. Sickening as it was, I stayed on for entertainments' sake. Olivia had been given a role in the town theatre. She was chosen as the leading lady for the fall show. Her family was of meager means like mine, but as an only child, the spoils were abundant. Sweet Aunt Sophie was a talented seamstress, but a homespun dress was never worthy to cover the splendid, Olivia Emory. She demanded the finest and Uncle Ross and Aunt Sophie always delivered.

After my interlude with "sweet" Olivia, I made my exit, exhausted from the falsity of our interaction. As I walked back towards the General Store, I laughed to myself as I thought about Olivia on Sunday mornings. With the cock of her head and a little shoulder shimmying she reminded me of a rooster as she strutted past Walter. Her tail feathers up all sassy like, and a smirk that was ever so despicable. Olivia Emory would never believe that Walter asked me, her run of the mill cousin, to accept his letters. I had no mind to tell her anything about it. The surprise would be worth the wait.

Celeste arrived a little late that morning. Her house was just a short piece down the road from ours. She helped Mama three days a week with chores and sometimes helped Daddy on the farm. Skin covered her in the darkest shades, and her eyes burned like embers of love. Her cheeks were full and sweet, holding a bright and friendly smile. Always carrying a kind word and a heart on her sleeve—Celeste was family to me.

Beginning the walk to school with my sisters when she arrived, I inquired, "Ms. Celeste, is everything all right this morning?" "Oh my, Ms. Gracie, our little calf got out last evening, and we were up half the night trying to get her back in the fence. I hope your Mama isn't gonna be mad," she sighed. "Mama will understand. She's done some cow roundin' herself, Ms. Celeste. Just don't you worry," I said, trying to comfort her. "You're probably right, child. Your Mama's a saint," she said grinning, as she waved goodbye. "Bye Bye

Ms. Celeste," we all cheered, as we made our way up the hill.

That woman had a way about her that warmed our hearts. Pippa Pearl used to say that "heartwarming" was Celeste's gift from God.

The walk to school was a little long, but we didn't mind. The air was fresh, and the scenery was beautiful. My sisters and I could talk about things, and I could daydream about Walter. When I tried to picture him at War, nothing came to mind. All I could conjure was the day he came to visit our home—replaying it over and over in my heart.

The eight o'clock bells chimed as we all jumped into our seats before they ended — little wooden desks all in a row staring straight at the front of that one-room schoolhouse. Ms. Pickens made her way to the front of the room and tapped her ruler on her desk. She had no time for shenanigans. It was serious business on her watch. "Class take out your slates and spend some time working on your morning arithmetic," she grumbled. I pulled out my slate and put it on my desk. Arithmetic was not exactly forefront in my mind. Thoughts of Walter on my morning walk still lingered. Not one to trifle, something overtook me. I begin drawing a heart with Walter's name in it. In a daze, I had no idea Ms. Pickens was peering over my back. "Gracie Emerson, what in this world are you doing? Since you're not interested in arithmetic this morning, you might like to recite Annabel Lee for the class," she said, as she took me prisoner. "Annabel Lee?" I thought. "It was Gracie Lee I had in mind, but I would give Annabel my best performance."

"Annabel Lee – By Edgar Allen Poe," I launched in with make-believe confidence.

"It was many and many a year ago,

In a kingdom by the sea,

That a maiden there lived whom you may know

By the name of Annabel Lee;

And this maiden she lived with no other thought

Than to love and be loved by me," I recited.

I continued with the poem, which flawlessly came to me from somewhere out of the blue. Annabel Lee had not even crossed my mind since the third grade and was hardly perfect then. It was apparent that an angel of mercy was handing me the lines one by one. I'm sure in part to punish Ms. Pickens for her vile attitude to all who entered her presence. Yet my heart told me that the angel may have been persuaded by Pippa Pearl. She knew I was in need of some divine intervention.

On a roll, I bellowed, "For the moon never beams, without bringing me dreams of the beautiful Annabel Lee." "That's quite enough, Gracie," stammered Ms. Pickens—stunned at the proficiency of my recitation. The classroom became full with smirks and giggles. Ms. Pickens had been defeated.

I proudly took my seat. The victor was a role I might love to play more often. Ms. Pickens grumbled as she instructed us to get back to our arithmetic.

In the bone-chilling cold of winter, I drift off into a world of dreams, on an island folly in the Mediterranean Sea. Love meets me there as I escape from the doldrums of life. It seems sometimes that true love might only exist on an island, for in the real world, love is painful, love is distant.

The fire flickers as I lay my head on the feather pillow and close my eyes. Lanterns lit for evening and family surround me. Captured in my fanciful thoughts, the loom of my heart weaves a story. I wonder if on my island Walter will be there.

I woke up from my slumber to Daddy's nightly reading of Robinson Crusoe, "All our discontents about what we want appeared to me to spring from the want of thankfulness for what we have," he quoted. I found many truths in the stories but enjoyed the romance of my own castaway fantasy. Robinson found content in the desertedness of his heart. He found a sort of solace, a coming to terms with God, as he embraced his helplessness as an island to himself. The marks he made on the cross each day were symbolic in so many ways. In some ways, those marks may have kept him alive. In other ways, he may have considered them marks of honor. He learned to become one with nature as he struggled to survive. And as others joined him on the island, he egotistically wrestled with his stature among men. While imperfect as he was, his time on the island became a catalyst for healing and finding peace with God.

I listened.as she spoke, "God's gonna do what God's gonna do, Ms. Gracie," were the last words I heard Celeste speak that day.

My feet shuffled down the gravel drive, as I kicked up rocks one by one, the aroma of the bread in my basket was so fresh I could taste it. One of Papa's loves was Pippa Pearl's bread. When she died, Mama started making an extra loaf to share with him. Carrying the treasure wrapped in a nice floral cloth alongside fig preserves, I made my way down the road to Papa's house. It was beyond my understanding how these little gifts could make him so happy, but I think in part, they reminded him of Pippa Pearl and how she loved him so sweet. "They had a special kind of love," I thought — one that Papa would never get over.

Hettie May was planning to marry Jon Peterson in the spring, and she seemed thoroughly content with the notion of it all. Jon was a handsome gentleman, a few years older, born into a well to do family in town. He could provide the niceties that Hettie May had longed for. Hettie May was beautiful and kind, but sometimes I worried that she might desire status above true love.

These thoughts made me wonder about love. What is love? Does love last? Could Walter really know he loved me with such little acquaintance? I wasn't sure about Walter's heart, but I knew mine. I knew that there was no one in the world like Walter Lee. I didn't know all the handsome, intriguing men on earth, but I knew that Walter had been permanently embedded in my heart. "There are some things you just know, Gracie," Pippa Pearl loved to say. I think she was right, at least for me. I wondered if Walter would change his mind about me while he was away. He might encounter some more interesting, beautiful women along his travels, which I feared would make me look simple and plain in comparison. He might wish he'd never come by the farm that day to ask me if he could pursue me upon his return. I stopped for a sit in the grass along the way to Papa's to ponder on Walter and our love.

"He loves me. He loves me not. He loves me. He loves me not," I whimsied as I tugged the petals from a daisy growing beside me. "Could love be that fickle?" I wondered. The final petal was drawn to "He loves me." I hoped my heart would settle in on that thought.

Each day as I opened my eyes, I knew in my heart that Pippa Pearl and Walter believed in me. Some days it was that feeling that encouraged my feet to stand to face the day. Their love reminded me that sometimes your cup does runneth over. But then, I wondered about those like Celeste, who may not have been loved as much as she deserved, but yet, she knew how to love people — so deeply and so freely. Pippa Pearl knew Celeste's ability to love was her gift from God, and she felt most loved when she poured her love onto others.

I approached the little white house in the woods surrounded by tall oak trees and wooden fences. Papa's lamb, Lilly, stood behind the fence as if to grin when I walk up to her. I rubbed her wooly head as Papa came out of the barn to greet me. "How's my, Gracie Lou?" Papa said cheerfully. I walked over and gave him a hug and replied, "Just fine, Papa." Papa and Celeste's husband Jim had been rounding up the cows for milking. They were both sweaty and soiled. "Would you all like some fresh bread and fig preserves?" I offered. They nodded in agreement and went to wash up.

In the misty morning light aglow, carolers raised their voices in heavenly tones as if to beckon the Christ child. The town was filled with a cheerful spirit. Children and elders alike welcomed Christmas Eve, perhaps, the most magical time of the year. A time when people could let go of their cares and think about something more spiritual. The gift the Magi received many years ago under that illustrious star.

Enchantment surrounded me as I made my way through the busy people passing by. As if to usher Christmas in, a single snowflake drifted slowly down in front of my eyes. In an instant, the twinkle of my lantern magnified its artistic design. Mystical and unique. A rare beauty fell from the sky. An elegant parade joined in — making their descent to adorn the streets.

The scent of bakery delights caressed the air as I approached. Pies, breads, cakes, and pastries galore were beautifully displayed behind the glass — ready to sweeten the Christmas festivities. Mama sent me with enough money to buy a red velvet cake and some assorted pastries. Mama was a culinary artist, but on special occasions, we got to enjoy the baker's fare. I pointed out to Ms. Cathleen just what I wanted. "Ms. Cathleen," I said, "how are you?" "Just fine," she said. "And how is Ms. Suzy?" Ms. Cathleen and Ms. Suzy were sisters, and neither had ever married. Both of them in the middle age of life had worked for their father in the bakery as long as I could remember. Mr. Bill Jenkins, opened the bakery before I was born, and had been there nearly every day of his life. Still in good health but growing a little feeble with the years, his daughters handled most of the day to day dealings. "Ms. Suzy is well," said Ms. Cathleen. "She's in the back frosting some cakes, but I'll go tell her you're here. She always loves to see you, Gracie."

Mr. Jenkins came around the corner with a sort of scowl on his brow. Daddy said Mr. Jenkins was ornery because he'd been in that bakery too long. Daddy thought he needed to take a little time off to enjoy and let the girls take care of things. The problem was, according to Daddy, he didn't trust anybody, even his daughters to run the bakery the way he did. But the truth was, Ms. Cathleen and Ms. Suzy, ran a tight ship and the store ran like clockwork, with or without ornery, old Mr. Jenkins glaring over their shoulders. Daddy said in the new year he would invite Mr. Jenkins out for some fishing. Sometimes, he said, "a little fishin' is just what the doctor ordered."

"Ms. Gracie! How are you, darling? Looks like you're out doing Christmas errands," said Ms. Suzy, as she made her way from the back of the shop. Ms. Suzy was as sunshiny as the new day. As ornery as her daddy was, she was that happy. Smartly dressed, petite and feminine, Ms. Suzy was taking care of business. Similarly, Ms. Cathleen was sweet and pretty too, but a little more on the quiet side. They both had a way with people. It was always a pleasure to pay them a visit.

After my short visit with the Jenkins, I gathered my goodies and headed out the door into the dance of flurries. Not minding the snow at all, I walked towards the butcher shop – where I was sure to find Daddy. Mama and the rest were at home making preparations for our Christmas day meal. I liked how I got to go with Daddy into town more often than the others. It gave me a feeling of freedom. And, most of all, I liked the people. Sometimes just watching them go by, but mostly talking with people like the Jenkins and the other shop owners. I learned about things in town.

Daddy had his back turned to me as I peered through the glass. Mr. Jake, the butcher, grinned at me nonchalantly. He knew I was up to something. I opened the door slowly, making sure the bell wouldn't ring. My hands were free. I had already put my goodies in the wagon. I tiptoed up behind Daddy and reached up to put my hands over his eyes. He jumped a little — slightly startled. Mr. Jake waited to see what Daddy would do.

Daddy stood as still, and as stiff as a board. In my mind, I knew he realized it was me. Mr. Jake didn't say a word. He just stared on with a quiet grin. I stood behind Daddy, with my hands still over his eyes. It became sort of a Mexican standoff. He didn't flinch, and neither did I. I couldn't believe how stubborn Daddy was. It must have been five minutes, and he had not moved or said a word. Still staring at Daddy's back, I had no idea what was going on in the store but was happy that Mr. Jake didn't have any new customers stopping in. After all, I was every bit as stubborn as my Daddy. My hands started aching from holding them up high. I closed

my eyes for a second to take a sigh and think about my next
strategic move when all of the sudden it happened. Daddy
and I were trapped underneath a giant burlap sack. It came
down so hard and fast we didn't even know what happened. I
dropped my hands to try and scrape my way out, and Daddy
tripped over my feet. Next thing you know we went crashing
to the floor – like a couple of cats in a bag, writhing around
the butcher shop. Mr. Jake laughed so loud the room shook.
I couldn't believe what was happening, and Daddy couldn't
either. We'd both been had. As Daddy pushed the sack off
of our heads and we made our way to our feet, in walked
Pastor Crain with a very puzzled look on his face. "Feeling
the Christmas spirit, are we?" proposed the Pastor. We just
laughed and said, "Why yes, yes Pastor Crain, we are."

Frost covered the ground like a soft blanket. My eyes hesitant to expose themselves, I pulled the covers back over my
head. In and out of dreams, I envisioned happy endings. The
morning light peered over my window ever so slightly, as to
not abruptly awaken me. It wasn't often that we were allowed
to sleep in until sunrise, but on rare occasions, Mama would
leave us to our rest while she read or did some knitting. I
think she enjoyed those times to herself when she could savor
her coffee and her solace in peace and quiet. Daddy usually
enjoyed his morning time by the fire, especially during the
months of winter.

Hettie May's special day drew closer. Plans for a spring
wedding were being made. As the oldest daughter, people
expected me to marry first, but I was content to wait until
the timing was right. Walter was almost like a fantasy to me.
While I knew in my heart he loved me dearly, and I loved
him, I didn't have anything to cling to. There were no letters.

No rings. No engagement. I couldn't even share my heart for him with friends and family. It was all so new. It was all so abstract. Eight months had passed since I had seen him, and my heart only grew fonder. I often wondered what it would feel like to see him again.

Since Walter left, I found myself changing – in little tiny ways. I wanted to be better. I wanted to read more and to learn more. I wanted to write. I wanted to know more about myself. I wanted to be the best Gracie Emerson that I could be, for Walter Lee.

The sun made its way to my eyes, gently warming them to the morning light. I tossed my head on my pillow and stretched my arms and legs in a cat-like fashion. Placing my feet on the floor to face the day, I stood in positive anticipation. As I entered the kitchen, Mama was tying off the yarn of a beautiful quilt she was crafting. She smiled to welcome me into her day.

I heard Celeste's words ringing over and over in my head. "God's gonna do what God's gonna do, Ms. Gracie." I wondered if she was right. Was there no amount of wishing, hoping or praying that could change God's plan? I often wondered about prayer and what its purpose was. Was it for us— or for God? Pippa Pearl always said that God knows every heart through and through. He already knows the prayers of your heart. I wondered if prayer was a way to hear and accept God's plan, and to align our hearts with His. Sometimes these things frustrated me, but I pondered them that day until my heart found peace. If God's plan is always God's plan, then I am in the very palm of His hand, and everything that happens to me, or around me, is how it should be. Somehow that notion left me at ease.

Ms. Pickens ushered us into the cellar of that one-room schoolhouse. It was a tight fit for all of us, but somehow we knew that we were where we needed to be. Sitting on my knees, I huddled down, with my arithmetic book over my head. The sounds of mighty winds blowing and wood clanging loudly captured my attention. Sadie wailed loudly, "Mama, I want my Mama." Peter held back tears, but I could hear him sniffling beside me as he shook with fear. I whispered to him in my softest voice, "Peter, it's going to be alright."

With shallow breath, I beckoned calm, as the roaring whistle sound approached. Louder and louder it became. Some of the children screamed. Those of us who were older comforted the younger children. By now, most of them were hysterical. Little Eliza was home with Mama since she was not old enough for grade school yet. "I love you, Gracie," Hettie May declared in a voice that rang of last word despair. As calmly as I could, I replied, "Hettie May, I love you too. We are going to be fine. Just take a deep breath and try to relax."

An hour passed as the building shook this way and that. In darkness the sounds were treacherous. The rain began leaking on our heads, and the thought of drowning in the cellar came over me. Thinking of escape routes, I would face the storm rather than die in the cellar. I asked God, "Please help me stay calm for the children?" All the while I wondered if Mama and Daddy were alright. And poor Papa, he was probably all alone.

Reflections of fall drifted through my mind. Another season had passed — another collection of memories for the books. I remembered the seasons of my life similarly. Sometimes they were cold and wintry. And sometimes I found them bursting with new life and new opportunities. Truly a time for everything under the sun. Like what I learned as a little girl from the third chapter of Ecclesiastes.

To every thing there is a season, and a time to every purpose under the heaven:

A time to be born, and a time to die; a time to plant, and a time to pluck up that which is planted;

A time to kill, and a time to heal; a time to break down, and a time to build up;

A time to weep, and a time to laugh; a time to mourn, and a time to dance;

A time to cast away stones, and a time to gather stones together; a time to embrace, and a time to refrain from embracing;

A time to get, and a time to lose; a time to keep, and a time to cast away;

A time to rend, and a time to sew; a time to keep silence, and a time to speak;

A time to love, and a time to hate; a time of war, and a time of peace.

Gracie began to emerge. Little bits and pieces of who I was. Some of the pieces went nicely together, while others found it difficult to fit in. Mama was beautiful, in every traditional sense of the word. But somehow, I always felt a little "controversial" in my beauty and other areas of who I was. Mama reassured me that my "uniqueness would make me better" and "help me grow." She often wondered aloud if Olivia would ever leave town or aspire for anything new.

For me, my beauty was never going to satisfy my heart.

Perhaps, knowing that helped me look for other places for my heart to go and grow.

Papa was a woodworker. Meticulously carving and creating with his hands. I loved to watch him work. The summers were when I enjoyed it most. He would tend to his farming chores in the morning, then Pippa Pearl would serve a meal for whomever was on the farm. Whomever, usually included my sisters and I. I loved her dinners. Green beans, cornbread, baked chicken, corn on the cob, sweet potatoes — just to name a few.

After dinner, Papa would rest for a little while in his chair, reading something of wartime chronicles or an excerpt from Kiplinger. He loved anything related to politics or business. Papa was a good steward of the gifts he'd been given and shared generously with those in need. His land was his treasure. He cherished it for what it offered his and future generations.

After Pippa Pearl died, Papa died a bit too. I noticed the little things first. Like how his face seemed to age a bit, and how his eyes lost their sparkle of hope. His relaxed gait began to stiffen too. These were just the physical manifestations. I imagined that they were symptoms of a broken heart. He still smiled and gave generously of his time to his family, but there was a looming sadness that I detected. I believe I saw in him, what I felt in me. I died a little too with Pippa Pearl. She was a source of hope and inspiration for me and probably in a small way, the world. There were days when I felt I might not be able to go on. I didn't want to die. I just wasn't sure how to live.

Along with the sadness, came the breaking away from woodworking. Papa was no ordinary woodworker. He carved things like forest and farm animals, crosses and flowers, beautiful things, so poetically. Mama had them handsomely placed all around our home. They reminded her of Papa and his love for nature and all things true.

I visited him one afternoon after my schooling and chores were completed and after he'd finished farming for the day. We shared conversation and tea on his front porch as we familiarly covered the usual topics. On the porch was a red bird carving. My favorite. And a beautiful blue bird. "Papa, do you ever woodwork anymore?" I asked him and interrupted before he could answer. "I just, well, (I hesitated) really love your work. One day we could take them to town to sell Papa!" I finished excitedly.

Papa continued staring at the white washed porch floor. It looked as if he were examining each little imperfection with care. I waited for what seemed like minutes for a response. Then he finally answered, "not much, Gracie." The tone of his voice and the lack of eye contact let me know he didn't want to talk anymore. We sat in silence for a bit longer. After a while, lingering in the uncomfortable air of silence, I stood to give Papa a hug and say my goodbyes.

On my walk home, I felt sad. I wasn't sure if Papa would ever be the same. He might have given up in some ways. I wondered how it felt to be on the "other side" of life nearing Heaven. "It must be a little scary," I thought. The unknown of it all. Celeste told me once when her mother died, "Gracie, God has a plan for people, on Earth and in Heaven. He isn't gonna just leave us alone." She was sad when her mother passed away, but she truly believed her mother was with God. Her faith was shockingly simple at times. She shared with me on occasions how her mother had a very hard life. Still, she knew she had to love people, even in the direst of circumstances, to be a beacon of light to others. She knew this earth was not her home. She knew loving others was her way to find some happiness in a broken world.

Reading from the pulpit, Pastor Crain was unusually handsome that day. I was definitely not in love with him, but a handsome man, so confidently reading from the Bible, captivated my attention. Pastor Crain had moved from the West a few years prior—the northern part of California. After sending letters back and forth with some relatives, he said God sent him here to plant a church. Pastor Crain brought with him a depth of knowledge of places and people that he collected along his travels. Sometimes he would make reference to the landscape and beauty of California.

Pastor Crain warned of the harms of alcohol but turned a blind eye for any who chose to consume. There were those in town who overindulged, but Pastor Crain, as far as we knew, enjoyed his wine in small quantities. He appreciated the robust flavors the fermented grapes offered.

Our family did not embrace alcohol. However, I found Pastor Crain and his interest in fine wines fascinating. It seemed my curious heart wanted to know a little bit about everything.

I glanced across the room after my daydreams of California, to see my sweet, sweet, cousin Olivia Emory, doing her best to preen, in the middle of the prayer. Olivia was still Olivia. Pastor Crain began reading aloud a verse from the book of Psalms when somewhere halfway through Psalm 54, Olivia's hair tousled and her eyes batted; almost in time with each other it seemed. I laughed silently at the site. Now that Walter was away, Pastor Crain was her next conquest in waiting.

Olivia became obviously ruffled, as Pastor Crain continued the sermon paying her no mind. It was days like this that I felt closer to God.

We headed out just after lunch. It was Saturday, so the afternoon was free for exploring and visiting. Mama made a little chocolate cake for Celeste. It was her birthday. I asked Mama how old Celeste was, and she said she didn't know, and that it was impolite to ask. Celeste always had a childlike appearance, but I knew she must have been as old as Papa, and he was in his seventies.

Never wanting to make a fuss over herself on her birthday, Celeste would say, "It's just another day. The only birthday that's important is Jesus's." But Mama knew that Celeste being born brightened up our world, very much. So on May 15th, we celebrated Celeste.

Celeste's house was a little piece down the road from ours. It was about a mile down the main road from our farm, then a left turn past the church and around the bin. We would go up the hill and way back into the woods. We didn't mind the walk. My sisters and I loved the chance to travel somewhere by ourselves, and Mama knew it would warm Celeste's heart. She and her husband never had any children of their own. Mama said, "Celeste's body wasn't able to make babies, but she gets to love everybody else's." And she did.

Kicking a rock off the road, Eliza's brown boots took two steps to my one. Her blue gingham dress fell below her knees in an A-line drape. I loved the way she looked. She favored Mama. Her eyes in a sparkling blue and her hair a golden blonde. Long and wavy, she usually wore long pigtails, but that day, Mama gave her special braids. Beautiful French braids, woven meticulously and falling down her back, with little white ribbons to polish them off.

Eliza loved Celeste just like the rest of us, but they seemed to have a special connection. In a way, Eliza embodied a little bit of Celeste. "Heartwarming" came naturally to

Eliza too. But for Eliza, it wasn't so much what she said. It was her eyes. She could warm people's hearts just by looking at them. Papa said, "she could soften a hardened criminal with one look." Perhaps her eyes were a reflection of her heart – warm and kind.

We made it to the church and turned off left. Behind the church was a beautiful batch of wildflowers. Hettie May never let anything beautiful evade her eyes. "Look!" she said. "Let's gather some for Celeste." We all agreed and selected some of each color to surprise Celeste with.

As we headed around the bin and up the hill, I couldn't resist. I started skipping and saying, "We're off to see the wizard, the wonderful Wizard of Oz." The girls joined in, "because, because, because, because, because – all the wonderful things he does."

Daddy had spent the previous spring reading 'The Wonderful Wizard of Oz' to us. It was the best book Daddy had ever read to our family. Each evening after supper we would wait for him to take his place in the den to pick up on the tale where he left off the night before. Captivated by Dorothy and her adventures, that story meant something to me – something to my family.

Continuing our walk, for a moment or so, I pretended to be Dorothy. Little Eliza was Toto, and Hettie May was Glinda the Good Witch of the South. Ginny pretended to be the Lion and Evelyn imitated the ScareCrow. I loved how Dorothy and her friends already had what they were seeking. I loved how they needed each other and their adventures to learn that.

As we crested the hill, the dirt road ended, and there was a little path back into the woods. We started down the path admiring the scenery. Celeste and her husband lived in a thicket. There was a creek flowing behind their house that made its way to larger waters.

As I looked up the creek, I saw Celeste kneeling down gathering some water. We went ahead to the front steps of her small wooden house and waited for her there. She turned the corner humming something beautiful that I had never heard. Celeste had a song in her heart. When she looked up, she saw us sitting there all smiles and beaming from ear to ear. "Happy Birthday, Ms. Celeste," we chimed in unison. "I'm gonna wear you all out! Nobody is supposed to make a big deal about my birthday. I've already told you girls that," Celeste scolded with a smile. "Come on over here and give old Celeste a hug," she said.

She loved her flowers and her chocolate cake. She told us she was going to hide it from her husband. "He doesn't deserve anything sweet," she said. Celeste showed us around her place, and we took everything in as we enjoyed our time. She had grown some peaches in her yard that she so generously shared with us. We enjoyed our peaches and our visit and then headed back out of the thicket for our journey home.

Months and months had passed — still no word from Walter. I was starting to lose hope that he would ever write. I knew that sometimes things that seemed too good to be true, were. Still, no one knew I was expecting the letters, but I suspected my family began to see a sadness in me. I became a little quieter and a little bit withdrawn. There was no way to sever the emotional connection in my heart. I knew for me to move on, I would have to write him a letter. A letter letting him know that I was better for having him in my life – if only for a moment.

Molly Wilson, a classmate from school, had a brother serving in the military. Her brother James was in the same company as Walter. I heard her talking about him to some

friends on her walk to school one morning. During class one
Thursday afternoon, I noticed her finishing a letter she was
going to mail off to her brother. On the envelope was the
address where their company's mail was received. I put my
hand over my slate, and as small as I could, wrote down the
address. I spent the rest of the afternoon memorizing it so
that I could wipe clean the evidence. My plan was to write
the letter that night at home and mail it off the next day after
school. I was a little embarrassed to be seen mailing anything
to Walter. People might talk. I would have to find a way to
get the letter out, without anyone knowing it was from me.

That evening after supper, I faked ill and went to rest in
the upstairs loft while Daddy continued with his nightly reading. I knew I had about one hour to write before my sisters
came up to bed. I thought over and over about what to say,
but every greeting and thought that came to mind was just
too trite. I knew I had to share my heart. I knew I had to let
Walter go. Circumstances can kill dreams, and dreams can
kill circumstances, but this time it was the dream that had to
die.

Dear Walter,

*I hope this letter finds you well. You are brave and beau-
tiful in service to our country. Your visit to our farm a little
over a year ago, deeply affected me. I have come to know
that sometimes people enter our lives for a reason, and
sometimes for a season. Your interest in me opened up my
heart. I have new thoughts on my place in the world and how
I want to try and make things better. While you are worlds
away from home, some part of you is residing in my heart. I
cherish you – and always will. I need to tell you simply, that
I am writing to release my heart from hope. The hope that*

your letters will come. I wish for you a life filled with joy and love; the fulfillment of hopes and dreams; a beautiful family; warm friendships, and most of all, the whimsy of life's simple pleasures. May God be with you as you continue along life's journey. And, If we shall ever cross paths again, I will be most delighted.

Very Truly Yours,

Gracie Emerson

The simple elegance was understated. A white steeple and a red door set the scene. Trees cascaded the perimeter of the country church. That's what Mama called it anyway. "Let's head down to the country church," she would say. I guess since we didn't go to the church in town or to Celeste's church, ours was the "country church." Pastor Crain presided nicely over the congregation and usually on Sundays wore a white shirt with his black suit of clothes. His hat was hand-crafted from black felt, and in gentleman fashion, he removed it before beginning the service.

It was the beginning of summer, and the landscape was lovely. I approached the church with my sisters. Mama and Daddy took the wagon, and they would let us walk if we left early enough. As we made our entrance onto the church landscape, I felt their stares. Their little eyes weighed heavily on me. I knew it was me they were interested in and not my sisters. It was always Gracie. They couldn't quite pin me down. There was a group of girls, mostly my age, and some of their mothers as well. They had probably rather spit venom at me instead of words. Words might have come out of their mouths. Even nice words - but venom was attached.

Just when I thought I couldn't exist for another minute of daylight, summer solstice arrived. As I wearily turned the pages of Daddy's Farmers' Almanac, I felt my heart disappear in a sort of momentary hopelessness. The spring had been the most beautiful season I could remember. Every living thing seemed to flourish around me, while I died a little each day. Some days, I wondered if I had been martyred for each blade of grass, for each budding blossom, for the berries, for the dandelion wishes. Beauty surrounded me with new life vigor. Yet, I had lost my desire to breathe. It was then I knew, God still provided just enough oxygen to sustain me. I hoped no one would notice that I had lost a willingness for hope. I did my best to mask the oozing, wounded heart that was trapped inside of me.

"Gracie, you have a different kind of heart. God has given you a gift. The gift to feel the pain in this world." I didn't know why Mama said these things or what made her think of them. I looked on her listlessly as she continued, "God needs people like you, Gracie. You're going to make a difference. A real difference."

I hated how Mama could read my heart sometimes. I thought I was better at the masquerade. It made me wonder if she'd had down times too.

Amber lifted our spirits. Day after day. Minute after minute. We'd had kittens before, and cats, of course, as any respectable farm did. The farm cat was a right of passage for the barn. It kept the mice population down and added a hint of mystery to the landscape. There were tabbies, and calicos, and black and white spotted cats of all sizes on our farm. When new babies were born, I would spend time trying to entice them out of their mother's hiding place with some fresh smelling food. Sometimes a tiny bit of cooked fish Daddy had grilled or a little cup of milk. If I could get them to come to the food, I could pet them once or twice every day until they became tame enough to hold. Some of them gave way to my persuasion; others did not. We gave each farm cat a name. "Animals deserve names, Ms. Gracie. They're gonna help you out on the farm. You might as well give them some dignity." Celeste was wise with her words.

So as each new litter arrived, we'd find them and peep in on the kittens. We would do an inventory, and my family and I would choose names for them. Usually, there were enough for me and my sisters and Mama and Daddy all to name one.

I picked up the scattered pieces of my mind and heart as I inhaled a tiny bit of hope. It wasn't as if anything had changed, really. It was a typical day: the clouds with a little light shining through every so often, and birds with their usual serenade.

However, I had been through something — a searching of sorts. A searching for a safe place to land, but there were none. If I were a bird, my wings would have become stronger from the frustrating flight.

And as a girl, my heart became stronger, too.

Through the search, I learned a little something about myself; that for me to survive in the world, I could never stop searching or find that safe place to land. And understanding this realization, was my safest "landing." The acceptance of living with the unknown was my first step to healing. In becoming more of the Gracie Emerson, God wanted me to be.

It was a Tuesday, and school was out for summer, so I was attending to my regular chores around the farm. They had become so mundane. I could almost do them in my sleep. I wondered how other people felt, how these simple things could satisfy their hearts for an entire lifetime.

I became frustrated with myself at times for not feeling satisfied with anything. Sometimes, to break up the monotony, I would make up silly songs to sing, daydream about the perfect romance, or think of places I would travel someday when I was older. I wondered if "those" people did it too. I wasn't sure. I had only assumed their simplicity. A simplicity sometimes I craved. I craved it for peace of mind.

So whether it was serendipity or divine appointment, on this Tuesday in mid-July, hope came to me. It wrapped its loving arms around me and reassured me that to dream is to live and that my dreams might be my purpose. And sharing them might help others too.

Daddy's friend shared some of his honeybees with us one summer. He came and set up the hive right there on our property. Our family loved honey, but Daddy had not yet learned the craft of honey harvesting. So Mr. Earl would come by once a week to check on the bees and do the necessary tending. A lot of days, the entire front of the hive would be covered layers deep with honey bees. I'm not sure, if they needed fresh air or if they just enjoyed the closeness.

Mr. Earl was older than Daddy. They had grown up together, and Mr. Earl had a brother James who was Daddy's age. James left to serve our country and continued to advance in rank. I think he ended up in California someplace. Mr. Earl would keep Daddy abreast of James' whereabouts so I would hear bits and pieces.

There was a usually a freckle-faced, toe-headed boy in the wagon when Mr. Earl came over to tend to the bees. I wasn't sure if I should hide when he arrived or not, but for some reason, my sisters were always busy with something else, so I was appointed his playmate for an hour or so, while the men worked.

His name was Peter. Cute I guess, with a mischievous sort of face. He was almost my age, but I was much taller.

It had been several weeks since I had made that dreaded trip to the post office to send Walter his release letter. I did feel better just knowing he might know how I felt. I dreamt that his eyes welled up a bit upon reading my letter, and wished that he would always love me in some way. These thoughts helped me begin to move on.

Along the way to school as my sisters and I approached town, Molly Wilson and Sarah Smith merged into our path for the last part of the walk to school. Sarah asked how Molly's brother was doing, and she reported that their family had just received a letter. "James and Walter have met some nice girls," said Molly. "Oh, really?" Sarah said. "I bet they are so beautiful. Do write your brother to send photographs soon."

My heart fell right out of my body. I continued walking, but Gracie Emerson lie dead right there in the middle of that dirt road. The feelings I felt were indescribable. I felt ugly, childish, ridiculous and insane. Followed by an enormous amount of rage. I was furious with Walter. How could he just toy with my heart like that and leave me waiting without a trace? In a way, I felt like I had dreamed everything up from absolutely nothing, but then I remembered his eyes that day. Those eyes told a story that could not be erased from my heart. Those eyes were honest. Those eyes loved me. Yet, here I was holding the "fool" bag. So frustrated I wanted to wreck the school-house and Ms. Pickens with it. "It's time for your morning arithmetic," she sputtered.

The scowl on my face was un-hideable. I hoped with everything in me that she would call on me. Unprepared today, It would be my pleasure to infuriate Ms. Pickens.

"Jack, would you please come work out the first problem for the class," she asked. As Jack proudly stood up with a smirk and made his way braggadociously to the board, I speared his back with my eyes. I would have kicked him in the butt if I didn't have to hear it from Daddy on arrival home. Jack, being an only child, must have been told over and over again that he was fantastic at everything on the earth, which was slightly and painfully irritating to me, especially that day.

He picked up the chalk with an obnoxious grin and quickly worked the problem. "Anything else, Ms. Pickens?" he asked. "Yes, a swift kick in the butt," I muttered in my mind. I couldn't believe how ugly I could be, but I was hurt, and I had to lash out if only in silence. I couldn't believe some other girl, was dating Walter. Oh, and all the things they might be enjoying together. Walks, and talks and dancing. No, not dancing. "Perhaps we shall," I remembered. That one hurt the most. "She got my dance. She got my heart."

Frustration followed me all the way home. I was so hurt, in so many ways, but mostly frustrated. So many emotions surrounded me, and the worst part was there was no one I could talk to. No one knew about my interlude with Walter. No one except Walter —and he was oceans away dancing and carrying on with a beautiful, fair maiden. There was no possible way I could sit at supper and pretend like everything was lovely. It just wasn't.

I made my way outside before it would be time to help Mama with supper chores. I didn't know whether to scream or cry, so I did nothing. I sat down on my special rock. The one that lay right in the edge of the woods, and put my head between my hands. I didn't think I would ever be worthy of love. Right there, I ask God if He even loved me. I just knew Walter had discovered I was too simple to pursue.

God didn't answer me. At least not in any voice I could hear. But for some reason, I envisioned Pippa Pearl. Her beautiful blue eyes and how they looked on me with love and I remembered how she believed in me. She knew I was going to do something. I remember how I had to write out my pain after her death. It was then, I realized, I would have to write out the pain of losing Walter too.

There were several places we would pass on the way to school. One of these was Mr. Greely's house. His little white house set just a bit off the road we walked along. It was a very modest home, with some magnolia trees that looked great for climbing. I would have stopped to climb occasionally, but everyone in town knew that Mr. Greely was a drunkard. I wasn't exactly sure what that entailed, but evidently, it meant an outcast that nobody talked to or even cared about.

We would pass by early on school days, and Mr. Greely would usually be on his front porch enjoying a cup of coffee and a book. I guessed it wasn't the Bible since most of the church people decided he wasn't worthy of love. But, each morning when our posse' would come into view, Mr. Greely would yell out "Good Morning! Have a blessed day!"

I wondered why the drunkard, monster seemed like one of the most amiable people in town. I just knew any one of us could enjoy conversation with Mr. Greely. I could see his heart in his smile. Perhaps the mornings were his good time before the evils of drink took him over.

I remembered what Pastor Crain had said about wine, and how he enjoyed it on occasion. And then how Mama and Daddy spoke of the dangers of alcohol. They didn't hate Mr. Greely, but they didn't exactly know how to embrace him. I wondered how lonely he was — trapped in the solitary world that defined and confined him. His wife had passed ten years or so prior, and they never had any children that I knew of. Mr. Greely became somewhat of a castaway of society. People would only speak to him if they had to when he came into town.

Daddy was a little different. I noticed he would actually make eye contact with Mr. Greely and tell him "Come see me on the farm sometime. I might need a little help."

Daddy believed in people — all kinds of people, and he tried to see the best in them. I think he had a little bit of hope left for Mr. Greely, and, so did I.

I had finally started to come to terms with Walter dancing with an exotic maiden overseas when Olivia Emory came into view. I would have just assumed to punch her between the eyes rather than say hello to her, but somehow I pulled out my usual greeting. "Good Morning, Olivia." "Good Morning, Gracie," she whined.

In every way, I was destroyed in Walter's dismissal of me, but I knew one other girl that had it coming too. I could see it in her eyes; she just knew when Walter came home, he would be ready to court her. I fantasized all during church that morning about a Walter homecoming. Would he marry that beautiful girl? I couldn't wait to see Olivia's face when Pastor Crain would announce the new couple in Sunday church. Oh, my heart would be shredded into one million tiny, little pieces. There was no doubt about that. But the one thing that would see me through and give me a bit of hope for humanity, was the annihilation of Olivia Emory.

In the evenings, the water made ripples on the pond behind our house. Watching them was a curious habit of mine. It seemed as though I had always done it — a time before this was out of memory's grasp. As the wind blew the water gently, I would count the ripples as they made their way towards me. Trying quickly to count them all before they reached the pond's shore and ended their journey.

In the blink of an eye, things can change. I had heard that before. I would never forget it. "Sometimes people die. They actually leave this world. From one moment to the next someone is living and breathing, and then, they are gone. Just like that. Sometimes with warning and sometimes without."

When Pippa Pearl died, I started thinking a bit more about Heaven. I knew I would never, ever see her again in my earthly life. The promise of Heaven intrigued and, in a way, fascinated me. The thought of living forever was something my mind couldn't comprehend. Poetry helped me. I think God sent me words. Little glimpses of Heaven. Pippa Pearl may have asked Him to. If she could help me – she would. I just knew it.

"Fanciful I fly. Through star-lined streets in golden hues. No Hellos. And No Goodbyes. It's nice to meet you."

(journal entry)

I guess I've never really understood people, any people. In trying to determine their behavior and why they act the way

The chord had been cut. Painfully and slowly severed.
Sending Walter my letter was my way of releasing my heart.
I often wondered, how it found him. And, how it left him. I
wondered if he would ever write back. These thoughts consumed me for several weeks after ample time had passed for
him to receive the letter.

It was on a Wednesday afternoon. I was heading home
from school with my sisters when I heard something in the
distance. It was the train. Its whistle blowing in an explor-

atory tone caught my attention, as it loaded up passengers for the upcoming journey out of town. Not knowing where their journey would end, in a way, made the daydream more mysterious for me. Seeking a sign or message from the Divine and wondering how and when I would ever let go of Walter — it was then that I heard the whistle blow. Something in my heart told me Gracie had to travel. I had to pack up my little bag of sorrows and take them out of town, sometime soon. As a symbolic gesture, if only to myself and God, that Gracie Emerson was moving on. I felt moved by the symbolic and poetic nature of it all. The thoughts of train and travel romanced me.

The notion of leaving town gave me a hope. I put Walter in the back corner of my mind and broken heart and begin thinking about my trip. Where would I go? How much would my travel expenses be? And, what would Mama and Daddy say? Would they even let me go? I could visit my Aunt and Uncle in the City. A real city, about six hours away by train. Aunt Phoebe and Uncle Gabe didn't have any children yet. Daddy's youngest brother, Gabe, was my favorite uncle. He and Phoebe had met in the city through a mutual acquaintance.

I hoped Daddy would let me ride into town with him on Saturday, so I could visit the train station and begin scheming for my autumn travels.

On pins and needles, all I could think about was my excursion. All day in the schoolhouse, I wrestled with my mind to hold its attention on Ms. Pickens and the lessons.

Tapping my fingers on the desk in a drum-like cadence, as in some useless effort to move time forward; the sooner the school day ended, the sooner I could head home and continue thinking about plans for my adventure.

The room became silent as I continued to tap. Watching my fingers in motion, I felt a mischievous smirk move across my lips. It was entertaining to me — this little secret of mine. No one knew about my plans to go someplace. I thought it best not to tell them just yet.

As I raised my eyes upward, there she stood glaring down at me with a snake-like gaze. I think Ms. Pickens had chosen me as her "prey" for the school year, or possibly for my entire educational experience with her.

"I expect that won't happen again tomorrow, Ms. Gracie," she hissed. "Now then, class dismissed."

I picked up my things and motioned for my sisters as we made our way down the road heading home. My sisters chirped all along about this thing and that, while I daydreamed about what clothes I would take along on my trip. I fancied we might go to the theatre, to dinner, or just around town. Whatever it was, Uncle Gabe, was a bit of a sophisticate. A handsome gentleman, with handsome taste.

The rest of the week came and went just like always; chores, schooling and time with family and friends. All of these, while avoiding the snare of the trap Ms. Pickens so skillfully set for me each day at school. I don't believe she'd ever gotten over the time she challenged me to recite "Annabel Lee." Her defeat that day may have possibly been the high point of my life.

Daddy and I left out early as usual that Saturday morning. The sun over the horizon was glowing, and the landscape was lovely too. But, still in the company of a seemingly perfect day — I felt tentative. My excitement waning. Only, I couldn't pinpoint a reason for my dread, unless it was a foreboding of sorts. A superstitious girl I was not, but I couldn't let go of the looming cloud hanging over me. Along the ride, I wondered about many things. If Papa were falling ill, or if my cat, Amber, had been taken by a fox or coyote or another predator. Many horrible conclusions crossed through my mind. Whatever the feeling was, I just knew something was wrong.

We made our usual stops into town and greeted the Wilson's in their store. After what seemed like the appropriate visiting time had passed, I left Daddy to make my way through the day I had planned.

My first stop was the train station. I was a little nervous that someone would see me there and wonder what I was doing. I had already planned what to say just in case anyone asked me. "My cousin from up north wrote me about coming to visit, so I'm inquiring about the schedule for her." I knew chances were no one I knew would be in the train station anyway. Most of our friends in town were shop owners, busy abiding to their duties. And then, the small town folks like us usually came into town only on special occasions. Daddy would buy extra supplies to take back to town for some of the smaller farmers. He said he didn't mind making the trip and saving them from the trouble.

I stepped cautiously into the train station with the intent to find out the schedule and fee for my autumn trip. As I stood in a rather long line, waiting to talk to the attendant, two very attractive girls, appearing a few years older than me, moved into the line behind me. Dressed smartly in catalog-esque attire, I was curious about them. Were they heading off to college? Or just going to visit friends? From their appearance, they didn't strike me as nurses heading out to service.

I fidgeted a bit while reaching for my papers and a pencil. I needed to make sure to have everything ready to take down the information needed for planning. A little nervous, I hoped I'd be to able to ask the right questions. Inching up a little in the line, I took in the panoramic view of the station, curiously making impressions of the place that I could remember.

I paid no attention to the girls' conversation behind me until I heard the word, "Walter." Looking back, I'm not sure if my shoulders jerked in surprise or if I stood a little straighter to pivot my ears back, but it was then I knew the cloud must have followed me right there.

"Well, have you heard from Walter Lee?" the darker haired girl inquired of her fair-haired friend. "Actually, I'm very disappointed. He was so kind and handsome that day. He told me he would love for me to receive his letters, and I gladly accepted. But, after all this time, I've still heard nothing," she explained with belabored breath. I could hear it in her voice; she loved Walter too. I slowly moved up a few inches and listened on for more.

"I just knew from the look in his eyes that he intended to pursue me. But now, I'm afraid he's met someone else. Someone more interesting than a small town girl like me," I overheard her go on in a small melancholy voice.

I couldn't believe what I was hearing. Those were my words — my thoughts. I wanted so badly, to turn around and chime in with my experience, but it wouldn't do any good. Besides, I didn't really want to look that beautiful girl in the eyes. I couldn't even hate her. Her whole heart was showing through in her voice.

The conversation about Walter was rather brief. I made my way through the line and asked my questions as appropriately as I could about departures to the city and details as they pertained. Making notes on my papers as I turned and slipped past the girls to make my way out. I couldn't believe it. Another girl, such a beautiful girl, had been swindled by Walter Lee. I wasn't sure if I should feel better or worse. Misery loves company I remembered; but there I was, still trapped in my silence.

As I walked through town admiring all the things I loved about it, I became angrier and angrier. The "humble" Walter Lee, who admired Gracie, and always had — was a swindler. A true swindler of hearts. I imagined the other girls he may have asked to receive his letters before he headed off. Were there two of us? Or ten? It was the honesty that got me. He actually counterfeited honesty. "Amazing," I thought. A man who can sell false sincerity is a dangerous man — a dangerous man indeed.

I pictured him that day, riding up so valiantly. I wondered how many other hearts he swindled that day before he left town. And then, there we were, all forlorn and heartbroken that Walter had never sent letters or responded. My thoughts went wild. "Walter must think he's special. He must think he's not accountable for the line of hearts he's slain. He must think God has given him favor on earth. God may favor Walter Lee, but Gracie does not," I continued in my mind.

I knew his type. He'd probably had everything under the sun go exactly as he wanted his entire life, but I hadn't. And, I understood why. It had made me stronger. Strong enough to forget about the "Swindler of Hearts," Walter Lee. "When I see him," I thought, "whenever and however that might be, I'm going to challenge him to at least look me in the eyes. Even though, I would much rather punch him square in the face than to look at him."

I wasn't sure what had happened. Everything I had assumed about Walter was now in question. I had imagined he was so strong and so full of love. I knew then, the man I was dreaming of, was a man of honesty and real passions. A man that takes accountability for his actions. All of them!

My life seemed to follow a storyline, often coinciding with the stories Daddy read to us in the evenings after supper. I wasn't sure what came first the chicken or the egg. Did I morph into the stories, or did the stories morph into me?

We had just completed the last chapter of "The Wonderful Wizard of Oz," which was my favorite story Daddy had read to us. Relating to Dorothy and the other characters very much, I wondered what it was that I was missing. Something that was a part of me all along. The narrative gave me something to think about.

Mama had prepared a delectable meal that night with chicken; fresh snapped green beans, corn and baked apples from our farm. Cornbread and banana pudding were also on the menu. After dining and helping Mama in the kitchen, we all moved into the den for our story time with Daddy. It was always a surprise finding out what our next tale would be. We hoped for the best since we would be a captive audience for Daddy, like it or not. We knew a little bit each evening could take a while to complete.

Daddy reached down beside his candlelit chair and pulled up something a little smaller than the last. With a presumptuous grin, he read more gallantly than usual.

"Through a series of misunderstandings, the secret love between Romeo Montague and Juliet Capulet, children of two feuding Verona families, ends in death."

That was his entrance — our clue. I could have wished for anything but a romantic tragedy at this point. I grinned as convincingly as I could. I still couldn't believe Walter, was the "Swindler of Hearts." After the events of the previous day, I was just furious enough to forget about Walter and move on with my life and now this — 'Romeo and Juliet.'

Daddy recited so poetically the lines of the characters,

which was moderately entertaining; I had to admit. I started to see a hidden romantic coming out in him. This was a little disturbing and a little endearing, all at the same time. Mama listened on with pursed lips and ladylike stature on the settee, as beautiful and elegant as ever. She seemed amused that Daddy has chosen something romantic.

Everything was moving along nicely, until Act 1, Scene 5 — the Kiss.

I could have gone the rest of my life without thinking about the kiss, the tragic kiss.

ROMEO

[To JULIET] If I profane with my unworthiest hand
        This holy shrine, the gentle fine is this:
        My lips, two blushing pilgrims, ready stand
        To smooth that rough touch with a tender kiss.

JULIET

Good pilgrim, you do wrong your hand too much,
        Which mannerly devotion shows in this;
        For saints have hands that pilgrims' hands do touch,
        And palm to palm is holy palmers' kiss.

ROMEO

Have not saints lips, and holy palmers too?

JULIET

Ay, pilgrim, lips that they must use in prayer.

ROMEO

O, then, dear saint, let lips do what hands do;
    They pray, grant thou, lest faith turn to despair.

JULIET

Saints do not move, though grant for prayers' sake.

ROMEO

Then move not, while my prayer's effect I take.
    Thus from my lips, by yours, my sin is purged.

JULIET

Then have my lips the sin that they have took.

ROMEO

Sin from thy lips? O trespass sweetly urged!
    Give me my sin again.

Often times, I would drift off into thought during Daddy's readings, and this time was no different. As I painted the picture in my mind of the sweet kiss of Romeo and Juliet, the characters came into view; only they resembled Walter and the beautiful, fair-haired girl from the train station. I breathed out a shallow sigh, hoping no one noticed. Something was telling me, she got the kiss. As I recalled her voice and her hopelessness about Walter, I just knew, she got the kiss. A kiss, she would never get over. At first, I felt a jealousy burning its way through me: those eyes, those lips. I imagined them so sweet.

How long would I mourn Walter had I gotten the kiss?

Was I better off not knowing its beauty?

Moments of clarity came as I remembered there would be no dignity in kissing the "Swindler of Hearts" — no dignity at all.

As Daddy continued on, I remembered that day when Walter came to see me. He took me by the hand to say good-bye. Only it didn't feel like two hands coming together. It was as if they were already one. If taking his hand was so beautiful, I could only imagine the tragedy of the kiss. Thoughts raced through my mind. Might the ending have been different had we kissed?

Daylight turns into night, Seasons come and go.
Life continues its merry way, While, the kiss, its ebb and flow.

It was over the next few weeks that things started to change. The essence of Olivia began to flail. Walter had vanished from my heart in so many ways, as I began the rebuilding of who I was, and whom I wanted to be.

Olivia, too consumed by self, had no idea that Walter had ever as much as crossed my mind, yet still; each interaction became colder and colder. An enemy moving in on me for the kill. Her nasty little eyes, transparently plotting my demise. Only, I wasn't sure why. Jealousy was the usual motivator, but I found it so unlikely. With my homespun dresses and tomboy quirks, I couldn't even imagine her concern.

As tradition would have it, Mama taught all of us girls how to sew as soon as we were old enough to hold the needle. First the needle, and then when our little hands were big enough she'd move us to her sewing machine — taking time with each stitch as to not put our fingers in harm's way, the needle moving its way up and down binding the fabrics and patterns together so neatly. Mama kept scraps in a basket next to the sewing machine for our lessons. Often, I would stare into the basket, admiring the many colors and patterns and how they complemented one other.

"The beautiful Gracie," echoed softly from across the room in a voice reminiscent of handsomeness. Thinking first, "there must be another Gracie," but in my heart, I knew I was the only one. Guessing then, I'd never thought of myself as beautiful. The Olivia Emorys of town were these.

On that day, I was wearing a dress I'd fashioned from Mama's fabric scraps. " I may be a painter or a writer one day," I thought, but my art of choice (and availability) was apparently, apparel. In hues of ocean blue, green and yellow, my dress carried on a natural feel. So different, in every way, than the usual frocks worn by the other girls, it was a daring move to even adorn it. In some ways, I felt free when I pulled it over my head and brushed it down over my hips. It flowed nicely over my curves, enhancing the shape of my body. Fitted to just below my waist and then flaring out into an A-line drape.

Befuddled by the voice, my mind could not reconcile its messenger. In a low tenor, that emanated just the right amount of understated confidence and sophistication – the voice was vexing.

As I made my way to the ticket counter, I decided the compliment had been given for another Gracie. Any Gracie, but me. The train station was full of unfamiliar, nameless faces. As I scanned the depot, I wondered which countenance shared my name. Was she fair-haired? A redhead? Or could she be dark-haired like me? Either way, someone thought "she" was beautiful.

Arrangements were coming together nicely for my autumn adventure. Uncle Gabe and Aunt Phoebe were busy making plans for my visit. It seemed they were excited to share with me so many things. Things I would be experiencing for the first time, and in a way, breathing new life into me.

On the way back home, my feet veered off the path and turned up the gravel drive to Papa's house. Sometimes I wondered if my feet spoke for my heart. I wasn't planning on a visit, but something inside of me knew it was time for one.

Walking up his drive, I saw him in the distance tending to his regular farm chores. Still handsome, I could see a smile light across his face, even from a distance. His hair was silver grey, with a little curl on the ends, still full, like in his youth. And, beautiful blue, grey eyes that spoke of honesty and goodwill. Papa was tall and lean in stature, as was most of our family. I often wondered if his physical beauty was just an extension of his heart. It shone through, naturally.

As I approached, Papa came into clearer view and called me over, as if to jokingly inquire, "Hello, Gracie, you been to the big city? You're looking mighty fancy in that dress!" With his kind jeers, he seemed curious about my appearance. After all, I didn't always traverse the farm in such. Feeling smart with anticipation, I responded, "No, Papa, not yet. Making plans for the big city though. I just returned from the train depot to reserve my tickets to visit Uncle Gabe and Aunt Phoebe this fall."

Surmising my dress a little more closely Papa quipped, "Did your Mama make that pretty dress, or did you order it from Sears Roebuck?"

"Good gracious," I grinned as I gave him a little slap on the arm, "You know Mama's been teaching me how to sew since I was wee little. I made this one from some of her scrap pieces. Don't you like it, Papa?"

"I'm just a simple farmer, Gracie, but I know a pretty girl in an uptown dress when I see one," with a warm touch to my shoulder, Papa reassured me in his usual way.

"Thank you, Papa. You know exactly what to say to a girl," grinning fondly, I hugged him. "Go on inside, Gracie. Get yourself something to drink. I'll be finished up out here in about a half an hour. Then we'll sit on the porch and solve the world's problems," Papa offered hospitably as he wiped his sweaty brow. "Don't mind if I do," I said, as I winked at him and turned to head for the house.

There was something about that house. Something that made it special to me. It could have been the whitewashed porch with hand painted rockers; or possibly the memories of dinners, of laughter, or of talks with Pippa Pearl. Or perhaps, it was the little trinkets they had collected over the years, each one with its own story. Some traveled from far away lands and others came from town, but as I looked at each piece, each special one, I was reminded of its story, as I recalled it. A wartime memento. A wedding gift. An Anniversary trip to the city. Or Papa's special carvings, with stories often inspired by nature's beauty.

After my brief trip down memory lane, something else caught my eye and my heart's attention — the beautiful upright piano sitting kiddy corner in the parlor. Memories as visions, of Pippa Pearl playing for us, captured my mind. She always looked so beautiful sitting there. Almost like it was an extension of who she was. As a child, her leaving never crossed my mind.

The dark mahogany wood frame of the piano was one of the most beautiful I had ever seen. Papa found it in town as a birthday gift for Pippa Pearl, not long after they were married. To add to its simple beauty, he hand-carved a vine of roses running up the left-hand side. Its one of a kind elegance almost took my breath.

I could nearly picture a younger Pippa Pearl, sitting tall and proper at the piano, with long brown wavy hair lining her back and enhancing the lovely dress she had made for the spring season. Moving away from her usual style, she let her hair down from the loose bun to a cascade of freedom. Perhaps, a representation of something deeper. Something that I would try to resolve years later.

"Come and sit with me, Gracie," her voice called calmly, but boldly in contrast. I remember being around six years old at the time. Grinning quietly, I went and sat with "my Pippa" (I called her) as she played Amazing Grace. Starting out a little soft, and ending up in a jazzy way, she took my hand and placed it on the notes a few at a time. I remembered her words, "Gracie, you're going to play piano one day. Don't worry if it's not exactly the way your Pippa plays it; you'll have your own way about it. Just play it from your heart, Gracie. Just play it from your heart."

I would never forget that day. Over the years, Pippa Pearl gave me little impromptu instruction, "middle c," "a scale," "sit up straight" and on and on. I knew bits and pieces about the piano, enough to try, but the timing had never been quite right.

(journal entry)

Today I ponder about life. It seems this is my favorite pastime as of late. It's an interesting plight, this life. You're born, and you find your place to fit into it. Some slip into life easily, so easily, it seems like they were meant for this earth while I feel a little out of sorts with the whole thing — the whole thing of living.

What if I were a cloud, I would feel everything exactly as I needed to, with no help of myself really. When it was time for rain, I would swell and overflow with the sweet letting go to the earth below. Some days I would evaporate and find myself taking on another form until I was beckoned to be painted white again. If only, I were a cloud.

"Gracie, are you frequenting the Feed and Seed for your dresses? That looks like a gunny sack you're wearing," Olivia hissed as she attempted to entertain her nasty little gaggle as I walked by. Unaffected, by her lame attempt to murder me, I stopped to look her directly in the eyes. "It's called originality, Olivia. Originality and style," I spit back as I continued walking towards the church steps.

Olivia had always carried a cynical, condescending undertone, but today was particularly if not outright, nasty and vile — a direct attack on my personhood. Pastor Crain looked handsome that day in his navy blue suit and crisp white shirt. The sun made its way in, softened by the stained glass windows, just in time to highlight and enhance his hair.

As I sat and listened to his reading that day from the book of Genesis, I couldn't help but wonder what made Olivia lash out so strongly. Jealously, crossed my mind, but I wondered why she would ever be jealous of me. Was it possible that Olivia craved something different? After all, different was what I was, and had always been. Sometimes I craved conventionality, but not in a fatal way.

My dresses were unusual. Mama usually had enough scraps for a dress or two a season. To add to the variety, I would travel into town and collect fabric scraps from the dressmaker's shop too. They had many nice size pieces that were only discarded or stored away. I offered to pay them something, but they always refused. I think they enjoyed my ingenuity. Sometimes when I would visit the shop, I would pick up on something to help in my dressmaking. The owners had immigrated from France years prior and still had heavy accents. I loved to hear them speak about Paris, the people, and its fare. Getting to know the Lafayette's had been a real pleasure.

As autumn came into view, the leaves began painting a scene so beautiful my eyes could hardly comprehend it. Brush strokes of amber, red, gold and the in-between caressed land and sky. It was in these times; I was reminded of the beauty of the Creator. The Creator of the universe — its natural rhythms and changing seasons. These thoughts brought me comfort through the changing seasons of my life.

The season of Walter had changed that day. Even in his death, I knew it would not end for me. It was a poetic ending — one of the most poetic I could imagine. Walter died as the fall skies were at their ripest. A beautiful epilogue. His body was on foreign lands, but his heart and his people were home.

As days passed by, the beautifully painted leaves began to make their descent. One by one they covered the ground in beautiful layers. It seemed, with each falling leaf a part of me was falling away too. I wondered if in some way they were little gifts from Walter to remind me of the beauty in the world. Or if they were little messages from God. Little symbolic pieces of Walter's body going into the earth. God knew what my heart could take. Burying Walter leaf by leaf was healing for me. I shed a tear for each one as fall made its way through.

Just days before my train departed and the passing of Walter so recent, I tried to pick up the pieces of my shattered heart and prepare to travel. Amber sensed something was wrong. She spent most of her time in my lap purring incessantly. With each hum of her purr, my heart felt a stitch of healing, like a Dr. repairing a severed heart. I wondered how she knew I was hurting, or how she knew she could help. Did God send her, or was it just in her nature? Either way, I determined, nature was God's too. So, God sent her. He sent her to love me and help heal me, a precious gift. Little things like this, reminded me of how personal He was.

As Amber and I embraced, words came into my mind. Beautiful words to describe the purr, the age-old purr that had healed many over the centuries.

An Ode to the Purr

The battalion hums through softness falls.
A thippity thump of admiration flows.
The timeless meander of nature's call.
As the purr, defeats its foes.

It was a cool, fall Saturday morning. My eyes opened more readily than usual. Wide open to what the world might offer me. Excited about a chance to see more of it, even just a small part. As I rose from my bed, I glanced into the mirror and grinned a bit at myself. Looking at my reflection was strange sometimes. At times, it seemed out of place, like someone else, I had not yet made acquaintance with.

My hair in a braid down my back with a few curls hanging around my face, I acknowledged some sort of beauty in myself. A beauty that I could feel myself in. My sisters were still sleeping, so I tiptoed quietly down the stairs to where Mama was. She looked a little tired, so I feared she was worried about my departure. We sat for hot tea, sweetened with a spoon full of Papa's honey, and talked about the day's schedule and my trip. Mama had not traveled much. In a way, it seemed that she never really needed or desired to. There was the occasional trip into town, or to the neighboring city, which seemed just enough to satisfy her. She seemed to know that what satisfied her heart might not satisfy mine. In some way, she knew I had to go and see, to travel and explore.

After tea, she stepped quietly into the sitting room, as to not wake the others yet, and returned with something that looked like a gift wrapped in beautiful hand painted paper and a bow, and her face with a soft angelic smile about it. "Mama, what have you done?" I asked her. "I thought you might need a little something to wear to the theatre or out to a nice dinner in the city," she said as she had me unveil the most beautiful evening dress I had ever seen.

As I took my place on the train, my eyes made their way around to familiarize myself with faces and place. Features of every kind and sort, I studied them for a good while. My mind wanted to guess their stories, who they were and what kind of life they had and were going to have. In a way, I may have sold some short and exalted others. It seemed that was how human nature works. We want to know where people fit in, in relation to us — a sort of pecking order. Feeling dejected by the Olivia Emorys of my time, I tried to find the positives in each person and each face, to dream a beautiful dream for them.

There was a serious looking girl. I guessed around my age. She had pale skin, dark eyes, and hair, with bright red lips, and dressed smartly and attractively, in a curious way. She held some papers in her hand, so tightly as if she were afraid to ever let them go. They were written by hand, which made me wonder if they were her stories or a love letter from afar. My mind dug deeper to fill in the blanks.

With Walter's death, a lot of things died alongside for me. The what if's of Walter were no more. What if Walter really does love me and will come for me soon? What if Walter's letter is on the way? In some ways, it was the "what ifs" that kept me going. Their death, in a way, killed me. "What ifs," represented a bit of hope on earth. Everyone needs a bit of hope in something. The journey to the city was my chance to talk to God about hope, and what to put my what ifs in. As I looked at the profile of the girl with the red lipstick, I could see a sadness in her face. It was as if, she needed to let go of those papers. In some way they gave her hope, and in some way, they were holding her back from something bigger, something better.

"Sometimes we cling so tightly to an idea, to something we need, that the joy of it is lost. The very love we had for it in the first place has vanished," I pondered. With Walter, he was gone totally and completely gone from earth, from my atmosphere. I hated it, every bit of it. But I knew I had met him for a reason and for a very short season, and in time I would know more.

My eyes opened as I moved from dream to reality. The steady lull of the train on the tracks and my still body rocked me to sleep. Mama always said I was a good sleeper, as a baby and even still. She rocked us to sleep in the evenings as babies and sometimes even after. The train must have reminded me of the nurturing love of my mother. I felt so free and relaxed.

As I begin to focus on my surroundings again, the people had not changed position or expression very much at all. Yet, it seemed I had traveled far away from them. In my mind, I had moved and changed immensely, but my body was virtually motionless. I wondered if their minds and hearts had traveled too.

I lifted my eyes to the landscape, and it almost took my breath away. The fall leaves were brighter and more beautiful now. The more north we journeyed, the more beautiful the view. The site of small towns, farms and all their trappings was so picturesque. I didn't have a camera but was hoping to save my money to buy one, one day. But, I did have a notebook and a pencil. Sometimes, I liked to sketch things I saw that inspired me. "I might write some things along my trip too," I thought. A travel journal. Yes, a travel journal.

The conductor announced only a half hour left until we reached the city. I began to feel a little nervous and excited.

As we made our entrance to the city, the countryside enticed me. The colors reached out to me. While exhausted from the travel, part of me wanted the ride to continue. I felt a freedom of sorts just being on the journey. With my pencil, I sketched a little bit of the train tracks on one side of the paper with trees dancing by on the other side. A simple drawing to remind me of my journey, yet there seemed to be something missing. My sketch was incomplete. I reached for my pencil again and opened the notebook back up. My hand hesitantly began to sketch a figure. It was of a girl walking alongside the tracks near the edge of the woods. Not knowing how or why, she began to favor the girl on the train. The dark-haired girl with the red lips and the papers in her hands. Sometimes my sketches seemed to take on a life of their own. I would examine them later to try and uncover their meaning. On first examination, this one meant something to me. It meant that the girl was going to go into the forest to let go of those papers. The papers, in some way, symbolized something that was holding her back. Something that was holding her back from being who she needed to be. I wasn't sure what her papers said or meant, but to my heart, the girl represented me too. My papers had lots of words on them. Some words that might have been false or hurtful, and some that may have broken my heart. Some that Walter left me with, with no explanation. On this journey, I knew I had to let my papers go, and let God make me into the girl he envisioned me to be. Without Him, I knew I would hold on to certain things for my entire life. "Gracie, God has a plan for you." I could hear Celeste's words ring true. Her words always comforted me.

Our train slowed as it pulled in closer to the depot. People started to rouse to a more upright position in their seats, taking note of their belongings and making arrangements with their hair. Onlookers began to appear in the distance waiting for friends and family to arrive.

Before I could close my notebook, my hand began to move. It wrote the word Walter in big letters. I knew I had to let go of my paper, for once and for all, before I could move on with God's plan. I wondered about Walter, and why he had to die, and why he had to hurt others. His kind face and smile could have been a guise for something undetectable, something God did not want for the others or me.

Even in death, I wished peace and love for Walter. In fact, I needed that reassurance. But even still, I questioned his intentions with me as I looked back. He had almost become an illusion. I wasn't sure if it was his pulling away of love that kept me in bondage, or his false sincerity, but either way, I knew it was time to let go of my papers and let God take up writing my story.

We came to a final stop, and I noticed on my watch that we had arrived a few minutes early. Happy in a way, I did not see Uncle Gabe and Aunt Phoebe. I needed time to find a place to let go of Walter. I waited in line behind the girl with the red lipstick. She stepped off the train, and so did I. She turned left, and I turned right. I walked outside of the depot and tried not to be noticeable in case my family had arrived. Slipping briskly down the beaten path, I found a little section of forest to hide in. I laid down my bag and took the paper I had so tightly held out of my hand. I looked at the word one more time. "Walter, Walter." How many times had my mind said the word, Walter? It was etched on my heart. I wanted it off. I asked God to show me how to restore my heart.

I took out a stick and dug a hole about four inches deep into the dirt. Then I took the paper and shredded it into a million tiny little pieces, dropping them one by one into the "grave" I had made for Walter. Once each piece had fallen in, I used the stick I made the hole with to cover them over. Then I took my boot and stamped on the pile of dirt to ensure its closure. A single tear drifted down my face. The symbol was from me to God. He would still have to heal me, but I knew His hands were with me as I dug — and as I buried.

I mournfully picked up my bag and headed back up the hill, trying to bring myself back together, ready to give a warm greeting. In the distance, I saw Uncle Gabe and Aunt Phoebe approaching.

Aunt Phoebe approached me as elegantly as ever. Her ways were unusually attractive. Petite features and build, she was simply and unmistakably pretty not even in a haughty way, but in a sweet way. Her eyes emanated kindness and openness. Uncle Gabe, a bit more gregarious, in his manner, walked with a confident cantor; almost adolescent-like. Somehow, the two of them just went together. What he lacked, she fulfilled. What she lacked, he fulfilled. Both quite enough on their own, but together they were a complete package of man and woman at its finest.

I wondered if I would ever find my true complement. It seemed such an impossible task. What were the odds that someone perfect for me actually existed on the earth? And what if my perfect mate was someplace like Timbuktu? I chuckled under my breath at the irony of it all.

"Gracie, you look all grown up, and so beautiful!" Aunt Phoebe never did hold back a compliment. "That's our girl, and adventurous too!" Uncle Gabe said excitedly. "We're looking forward to showing you around our city for a few days. You're going to love it."

Still, a bit of sadness loomed over me. My heart felt heavy and a bit lonely. Burying my papers of Walter and thinking about a perfect connection of souls, made me a bit sad. But as we headed away from the depot and rode through the beautiful countryside, I felt a peace come over me. The city began to emerge in the distance, something different than my eyes had ever seen before. Somehow the anticipation of life outside of home gave me hope. I exhaled and told God to take my present and my future too. I knew this trip was part of His plan. I took out my journal.

Leaving on a journey. A journey of discovery. The discovery of hearts that need healing and aspirations to unfold. Poetic gestures ignite into hopeful anthems while sharing becomes the catalyst for inspiration. Inspiration sends forth dreams. And dreams culminate into something higher, something noble, something born of destiny. As paths mingle, their purpose becomes clearer. Clearer for those who seek it. Each day a proliferation of hopes. Step upon step, day upon day, an eternal exploration — His mysteries unfold.

Emerald green. I wondered if it was the most beautiful color I had ever seen. As I slipped the dress over my head and looked into the mirror, I almost cried. Mama could rival any catalog or couture dressmaker. It was a perfect fit. Simple in its elegance, the ebb and flow enhanced my curves in an ever so appropriate way. And with a just right satin, its shimmer added light to my face, enhancing my features.

I had never noticed the green in my eyes before that evening. There was truly something about colors and beauty. Mama knew it. She wanted me to shine. She truly did.

With a little time left before dinner, I sat on the bed to wait for a bit, not wanting to disturb Aunt Phoebe and Uncle Gabe. I couldn't help but think about my papers. I started to accept that there were other things written besides Walter and the circumstances that may have hurt me. Other things that God was going to reveal to me over time. Things I was responsible for too. I started to see that God doesn't just wipe the papers clean in an instant. His grace, sufficient indeed. Yet, the revelation of how mangled and battered the papers were could only come after turning them over to Him.

As I sat on the bed, a word came into my mind. A word I was too busy to notice when Walter was written so large in the center of my manuscript. The word was "grace." It was there all along, written in some sort of indelible ink perhaps. But God had underwritten all the corrupt and painful phrases that were human scribed with one word that trumps them all. Grace. I began to hum as I remembered the hymn.

Marvelous grace of our loving Lord, grace that exceeds our sin and our guilt! Yonder on Calvary's mount outpoured, there where the blood of the Lamb was spilt.Grace, grace, God's grace, grace that will pardon and cleanse within; grace, grace, God's grace, grace that is greater than all our sin! Sin and despair, like the sea waves cold, threaten the soul with infinite loss; grace that is greater, yes, grace untold, points to the refuge, the mighty cross. Dark is the stain that we cannot hide. What can avail to wash it away? Look! There is flowing a crimson tide, brighter than snow you may be to-day. Marvelous, infinite, matchless grace, freely bestowed on all who believe! You that are longing to see his face, will you this moment his grace receive?

When I woke, there was something different about me. Something different about the very air I breathed. My mind questioned the absence of dread. That trace of doubt and hopelessness that had followed me for quite some time. Had it lost its grip on me in the night, or had an angel fought it in my stead? Either way, at least for a moment, it was gone.

As my eyes opened a tiny bit wider, waiting for the sun to rise, thoughts of dreams began to surface. It was the voice from the train depot. In a dream, he approached me. Only, his face not yet visible. There was something comforting about the voice. Something familiar, yet brand-new. I couldn't re-call what he said, or if I said anything at all, but the voice let

me know I wasn't alone. It spoke of new beginnings.

That morning was unusually cold. Feeling exhausted from my travels, the return to real life was not effortless. It was Saturday morning chore time. I enjoyed the Saturdays going into town with Daddy more, but chore days were part of the routine. After breakfast, we went outside to do our part. It was my turn to weed the garden. In the fall and winter months, the garden was a little less trouble to tend, but the weeds didn't vanish. I often wondered why weeds seemed so hardy. I would pull them one day, and they could almost grow back by the next. It seemed there were some parallels in life too.

The sun barely up. We all did our part in the feeding, cleaning, weeding and caring of our farm, the farm that sustained us, and in some ways others around us. Farming was a way of life for our family — a way of life complete with lessons for the young to learn and the old to teach. The land taught us a lot too. "The land doesn't need a farmer, but the farmer needs the land." Celeste could take something so complex and simplify it in a way, that your memory could not let go of.

As I knelt down capturing each weed from the ground, I enjoyed getting them from the root. It was almost like a game; I challenged myself to leave no roots behind. I thought a bit more about what Celeste said about the land, and how Daddy and Papa took such good care of it. Rotating their crops and tilling the soil in as natural of a way as they could. The land was owned by our family, but ultimately it belonged to the earth and to God. Daddy knew some years the crops wouldn't yield as much for different reasons and different seasons, but he was still honest in his farming. He didn't overwork the soil or over plant. He knew that there was an ebb and flow with farming, and he was a good steward of his resources to account for the off years. "God's gonna provide, Gracie. He always does!" Celeste was walking towards me as I pulled the final weed from the garden. To Celeste, the garden seemed as spiritual as the church where she worshipped, and in a way it was. Being in touch with every element and natural way, trusting totally in something as old as time. What could be more spiritual than that?

"New beginnings aren't going to come easy, Ms. Gracie." Sometimes Celeste just had a way with words. It seemed as if she spoke to my heart, even unexpectedly.

School had let out for summer, and I had completed all the schooling that the one-room schoolhouse and Ms. Pickens had to offer. Papa had been woodworking all year, creating some of the most beautiful pieces I had ever seen. Daddy and Celeste's husband were planning to tend the farm for a month or two while Papa went on a little excursion from town to town selling his crafts. I was a little surprised when he asked me to join him.

I needed to leave town for a while, to think about who and what I wanted to become. I felt a little out of sorts. I felt a little out of place. Mama encouraged me to go. She thought it would be a nice journey for Papa and I. I think she knew we both had healing to do of different kinds.

We were to leave on Saturday, so I asked Daddy if I could go into town with him on Friday afternoon. I wanted to purchase a new journal and some pencils with the money I had saved. I started to see this trip as a place to explore my writing. Pondering life seemed to be a favorite pass time of mine.

A bit before sunrise, Papa and I pulled away from the farm. Neither of us said much. Silence had become comfortable enough between us. Celeste was right, I thought, new beginnings don't come easy, but for me they were necessary. Leaving the farm I loved, yet felt tied to, changed me in so many ways, as well as my trips into town with Daddy and my visit to Uncle Gabe and Aunt Phoebe. Every time I left, a new story was written in my book and a new twist of possibilities of who I was started to emerge.

About half of an hour into our journey the sun started to peek over the hill. A beautiful shade of terracotta, slowly becoming brighter as the sun peeked to its position in the sky. The land lush and green, with just the right amount of foliage, sprinkled with wildflowers and dew. Papa looked over at me and grinned still not ready to speak. I grinned back took in a panoramic view of what was ahead.

For a minute I wondered what everyone was doing at home, what they were saying about Papa and me. "Were they excited for us? Would they do something a little out of the ordinary today because we took a step into the unknown?" I didn't know, but I missed them all so much. My sisters, Mama and Daddy, and Celeste. Oh, and Amber. I loved them all so much. They were dear to my heart. But I knew this trip was meant for Papa and me alone.

Papa stared ahead, but the look on his face was pleasant. It let me know that he was open for conversation, so I proceeded. "Papa, where is our first stop? And, how long will it take us to get there?" His eyes moved up and side to side as his mouth dimpled on one side. I knew this meant he was thinking. "Well, Gracie, let's see, the last time I made this trip was ten years ago, so I believe we'll be a little faster now, seeing as the roads look a little better and all. So my estimate

is around six hours until we reach Little Green." "Papa, what
is Little Green like? Do they have a General Store? What
about a Bakery?" My mind ran in circles painting pictures of
Little Green and what it might be like. I couldn't wait to get
there.

*Little Green. Little Green. Will I find you in my dreams?
With meadows bright and cattle low. And smiling faces
dancing so. Little Green. Little Green. Will I find you in my
dreams?*

Holding my journal in my hands, I was so excited; I had
to write. I could only picture what the countryside of Little
Green might look like. For some reason, the town was elusive
to me. I think I was hesitant to envision it. I might create it to
look like our town or the one I visited with Uncle Gabe and
Aunt Phoebe, in a way, I wanted Little Green to be a surprise.
A wonderful little surprise.

"Papa, what are we going to do when we get to Little
Green? Do you know anyone there?" I asked as if it were my
job to make sure our accommodations were taken care of.
Mr. Wilson's brother Lee owns the General Store there. He
said we could stay in the loft above the store for a few days
and sell out front from the wagon," Papa answered me in an
assured voice. My mind went whirling about the General
Store.

I surprised myself. Thinking about Little Green and our
journey had taken over thoughts of Walter and everything
that had happened. I felt at peace about my hurt. It being a

part of me made me appreciate what was to come and where I had been. Had I not met Walter and experienced the flood of emotions that I did, I don't know if I would have been willing to embark on the journey with Papa. In so many ways, I still loved Walter and always would. I might never know the reasons for everything or anything, but Walter's life was not in vain. I knew, his life had made an impact on so many others and would continue to over the years. I knew God could use every breath, every mistake, every wish and every step of Walter Lee for His Kingdom. This thought was reassuring to me.

The barns we passed along the way didn't look much different from the ones on our property or those of our neighbors. And the people we passed and waved to looked a bit like us too. At a glance, people and places didn't change very much. No matter where we went, people had their struggles, but they still greeted us with open arms.

Papa stopped off at a small trading post called Harper's Point to give the horses some water and take a stretch. "Gracie, get out and stretch your legs, and, while you're up, go inside and get something to drink and a pastry," Papa suggested. He made his requests with authority like he knew the ins and outs of traveling. I got out of the wagon and meandered my way around the side of the post, stretching in a cat-like way. I was a tiny bit sore from the bouncy ride. When I opened the rickety door, there were two older men — one behind the counter and one in an old wooden rocker. They smiled as if they were excited to see someone more youthful. I grinned back and nodded my head to the side a bit, feeling shy from the attention. Papa walked in just after me. "How are you fellows gettin' along today?" he asked. "Doin' better now, since you brought this pretty young lady by to see us," the older man said. I turned three shades of red and said "thank you," as I walked to the pastries and picked up an apple pastry and some iced tea.

After the horses were watered and rested, and we'd had a nice stretch and refreshment — we said our goodbyes. The men smiled brightly and waved as if our visit made a joyful imprint on their day. In my mind, I knew it might take hours before another traveler passed through, but the men seemed content to wait. "Patience is a virtue," I thought.

The road from there was a bit smoother and the dust had settled some too. Everything looked so fresh and alive. I wondered if they had been blessed with rain. As we rode along, I remembered the Irish Blessing Daddy had taught us all. I wasn't sure why, but I think it was the familiarity of the "road"; something about it was poetic and beautiful to me. The way it narrowed ahead as it curved into a wooded area: the green grass and wooden fences framing its way.

May the road rise up to meet you. May the wind always be at your back. May the sun shine warm upon your face, and rains fall soft upon your fields. And until we meet again, May God hold you in the palm of His hand. ~ Irish Blessing

As I rehearsed the words in my mind, I thought about Little Eliza. She had a special place in my heart. It made me think that, in some ways, we were all "Little Elizas" to God. He truly holds us in the palm of His hand – even Olivia Emory. These thoughts made me feel so loved and so angry all at the same time. How could God love Olivia? That realization made my love feel cheapened.

Papa stared straight ahead looking forward in a serious thought like gaze. He must have been thinking about Pippa Pearl, or missing her so much, but either way, I was glad he didn't turn his head to look at the grimace on my face that must have been there for a half an hour or more.

God was working on my heart. I knew it. I knew he wanted me to put myself in Olivia's shoes for a little while, at least in my mind. Being Olivia was different from being Gracie. It always had been. She was the only child. I was the oldest of five sisters. Her parents gave her everything; ours gave us what we needed. She was beautiful; I was attractive in some sort of unusual way.

(journal entry)

If I had Olivia's life, I would be just like Olivia. And, if she had my life, she would be just like me. We are exactly who we are for a reason. Neither one exactly better, or worse. As I painfully think through my issues with Olivia, I know, I have been closed off to her, even as a little girl. I felt like an outsider. I knew I could never be like her, so I begin closing down the relationship. I realize now that I may have hurt her too. And perhaps, there were things about me she wished she could be like too. She began to see me as the outcast, and I saw her as conceited. We created a great divide between us, which I am beginning to see spread throughout our little "society."

I basically despised Olivia and all her friends. God was telling me to try to bridge the gap because they despised me too. I didn't play by their rules, and to them, that was threatening. To me, their rules were scary and debilitating. We just didn't understand each other. I didn't feel that the relationship was worth mending, but God told me it was. There was something larger at stake, and one of them was Little Eliza.

As we rode along the open road for a few hours more, I

thought and thought about how God might want me to begin mending the relationship with Olivia. I could only reconcile two courses in my mind. The first was to totally change who I was and try to be more like she and her friends. They might accept me if I gave up on being me. The second course that occurred to me was to totally let go of the relationship and destroy them by being the best Gracie I could be "without their approval."

I began to see that Olivia and her friends behaved the way they did because it worked for them. They felt good, felt honored, felt right. Anything outside of that system of beliefs was not good to them. They could not exist outside. I threatened them, and they wanted me to feel bad about it, bad enough about it to change, to die, at least inside, and to never fulfill my purpose.

Having friends was important to me, but not in the same way. My friends were people like Celeste, and Papa, and Mr. Greely and my sisters and others who I could say hello to, talk to about fun things or learn about the world around me. I didn't love the tight grasp of friendship that Olivia enjoyed. And I did not understand it.

The sun was setting in a beautiful amber red. I felt a peace come over me as we made our way into Little Green. The farms behind us were beautiful. The streetscape ahead, inviting. The silhouettes painted a beautiful scene of the town as the sun went farther down.

I asked God to help me get closure on my thoughts before we made our way into the General Store to make acquaintances and get settled in for the night. I felt something telling me to release the relationship. To let go of it completely. In a way, there was no relationship at all, but I was hanging on to feelings of insecurity and bitterness, bitterness for not being accepted. Yet, I didn't really want to be accepted by them.

Just before dinner, we began closing in on the town of
Little Green. The streetscape was more appealing than I had
even imagined. Storefronts in different colors with a charm-
ing essence. Benches along the way for resting and visiting,
and delights in view from each window. Every store seemed
to take pride in the details of how their shop appeared from
the street view. As we pulled into Mr. Lee Wilson's store and
tied off the horses, lanterns began to light. It wasn't quite
dark yet, but the sun had begun to make its way down behind the buildings. Its iridescent glow on the windows made
everything shine in such a beautiful light.

"You're just in time, You're just in time," repeated a
childlike voice from behind as we made our way out of the
wagon. As I turned to see the voice, I saw the cutest little boy
with freckles across his nose and bright red hair shining from
his head. I guessed him to be about nine years old. "You're
just in time for dinner," he completed. Papa smiled, and said,
"Well, young man, it would be our pleasure to join you, and
who do you belong to?" "I'm Mr. Lee's Grandson, Willie."
Mama and Daddy let me stay here in town on the Saturdays
to help Granddaddy. Come on inside." "Don't mind if we
do," Papa replied with a hint of excitement.

We walked into the General Store. It smelled of cedar,
herbs and fresh-baked bread. I saw a lady peeping in from a
back galley door. She smiled when she saw us and went back
in as if to finish preparations for our meal together. Mr. Lee
Wilson walked up in a cheerful, confident way. He stopped
when he had come close enough to give us a good once-over
followed by a smirk and a hug. It had been years since he had
seen Papa, and he had never met me. I could tell, Papa was
someone Mr. Lee enjoyed, as did most people.

"Well, how was your ride," he inquired of Papa as they

walked back outside to gather our things and water the horses. "Good. I really can't complain. We left out early this morning. The weather was beautiful, and the ride was pretty smooth. I really enjoyed being on the open road. It was a refreshing change."

"I'm so glad, you all are going to spend a few days with us, and I look forward to seeing your carvings tomorrow. We'll find a nice place for you to set up shop. Now, I bet you two are hungry from a long day of traveling. Elizabeth has been busy making a nice dinner. It should be ready to eat shortly," said Mr. Lee.

"That sounds wonderful; I'm going to go clean up if you'll show me the washroom. Gracie, you may want to as well," Papa licked his lips subconsciously, I think in anticipation of the supper in our near future.

As I looked around Papa's side, I saw Willie grinning at me, as if he would like a playmate. I winked at him as I made my way up the stairs to wash up and put my things away. He skipped back into the kitchen in the cutest way I had ever seen — his suspenders in a bright red to match his hair. There was something about him I liked.

We passed each dish around until our plates were full. Mashed potatoes, corn on the cob, beef roast, green beans, and fresh bread filled my plate. The foods were still hot from cooking, so the many aromas blended and made their way to my nose. I sat across from Willie. Papa was to my right. Mrs. Wilson was to my left, and Mr. Wilson sat at the head of the table.

The conversation ebbed and flowed nicely like we were family or close friends. They wanted to know all about our family; my sisters, Mama and Daddy, and about what happened to Pippa Pearl.

Willie made faces at me all through dinner. "Gracie, have you completed school?" Mrs. Wilson asked as I finished a bite of mashed potatoes. Just about to answer her, I raised my head and saw Willie staring at me. His eyes large and his lips pursed, I almost giggled out loud. Holding back my nervous giggle, "Yes Maam, I completed my schooling this year. I may look at college, but I wanted to take some time with Papa to travel before I make any plans."

There was something about the Wilsons and Willie that I liked. They just seemed good-hearted, open and kind. I guess I generally liked most people. I learned things from them. Mrs. Wilson was a pretty lady— a dark-haired beauty.

The comfortable feeling of the store and their dining room made me feel right at home. Every time I raised my eyes from my plate of food, Willie's eyes met mine. So quickly, I'm not sure if he had ever looked away. It should have made me nervous, but for some reason, I found him entertaining. Other than a few jester-like remarks and hm-mms over the food, Willie remained quiet all through dinner. Eating from the edge of his seat, he appeared as if he had someplace to be.

After we completed the meal and had a dessert of delec-table fresh-baked apple pie topped with the fluffiest whipped cream, I helped Mrs. Wilson carry the dishes to the wash-room and helped her with the cleaning up. Willie stayed in the dining room where Papa and Mr. Wilson were talking and laughing about old times, but it seemed that every time I turned my glance towards the swinging doors, they would close abruptly, and a little hand would disappear to the other side. I didn't want to feel vain, but if I was not mistaken, Wil-lie was smitten with me.

As I washed the dishes and helped with other tidying around the kitchen, I thought about what I might do when I was finished.

"Thank you so much, Mrs. Wilson, the meal was delicious. You are such a gracious host to have us," I said, offering up my best thank you. As I walked through the swinging doors back to the dining room, Willie appeared to be busy looking through a book across the way in the General Store. His eyes looked large and alert, and his face was smirked. I had a feeling it was all for show. Taking the bait, I made my way across the wood pine floors to the storefront. "What are you reading about, Willie? Something interesting?" I proposed so seriously. "Actually yes, ummm, it's about the Grand Canyon," he offered back. "Really, the Grand Canyon? That's a place I'd sure like to go." I said. "Me too, Gracie! One day, I'm really going to go there. You wanna see some photographs the man took? He comes by here once or twice a year to bring Granddaddy some books to sell in the store. He takes photographs and writes stories all about his travels." Willie chirped excitedly.

"Why Willie! You sound like a real explorer at heart." I grinned and winked at him as we thumbed through the book and he showed me the photographs and their stories.

That evening as I laid my head to rest on the feather pillow and wrapped myself in the soft blanket that would swaddle me to sleep, my eyes made their way around the moonlit room. I could see Papa's cot on the other end, and it wasn't long before he began to hum a little snore. Its cadence wasn't even disturbing. Actually, it reminded me just enough of Amber's purr. I had forgotten how much I missed her already. I wondered if she was cuddled up with Eliza or one of my other sisters and if she even missed me at all.

Thoughts of the evening and of Willie made me smile just

a little. In a way, even little Willie had inspired me. I remembered my trip to see Uncle Gabe and Aunt Phoebe and how it had opened up new horizons for me. The Grand Canyon was something so beautiful that I would have to see one day – just like Willie. I thought about how spending time in the store and seeing those books had changed him forever. I wondered if our visit there might change me forever too. I thought about Willie's freckle-faced grin and wondered why the attic loft felt almost like home.

One thought drifted into another as I drifted deeper and deeper into a peaceful sleep. The last thought I could remember was of the voice in the train depot. It haunted me in a kind of beautiful way. Its mystery had captivated a little bit of my heart.

The sun rose gently to my eyes as the smell of fresh baked concoctions made their way to my nose. I slowly moved my way up, as I heard Willie skipping through the store. It sounded as if he had never even gone to sleep at all. I needed a little more time in the mornings to gain my momentum for the day.

I noticed Papa was gone and his cot was already made. He must have slipped out early without me even noticing. The farm life had its ways of making early risers. As I slipped into my clothes for the day, the usual, except for a patchwork skirt I had made from some of the scraps from the dressmaker's shop near home. The colors and patterns looked so beautiful as the soft morning sun shone in on them through the attic window.

I laced up my boots and headed down the wooden pathway of stairs to join the others, and as I made my way to the kitchen, I caught a glimpse of a little yellow dog outside of the window wandering around on the front porch of the store. I wondered if it belonged to the Wilsons.

Mrs. Wilson had prepared a wonderful breakfast of fresh

pastries, poached eggs, and fresh fruits. A little different from what I was used to at home, the food reminded me that I was someplace else.

It wasn't long until Papa, begin setting up his wares outside of the Wilson's store. The long wooden table was covered with beautiful wood carvings of all types. I began to notice that day how Papa's art had become even more beautiful. It seemed he was putting all the hurt from losing Pippa Pearl into each and every piece. It was almost like a memorial of her beauty and love.

The journey was a turning point for Papa and a new start for me. To me, Papa taking the trip signified his decision to live again. He needed to create. He needed people. And, I would find out later that the people needed him and his creations too.

It was a sunny day with a nice sprinkling of clouds in the sky, and Papa was expecting at least a few passers-by. I don't think he worried as much about selling the items as he did about enjoying the company of complete strangers.

Soon they began to come. Most would stop to at least say hello and admire Papa's work while others would stop and purchase a carving for themselves or a loved one. He knew people did not have an abundance of money, so he sold his wares at prices the people could afford.

I peered across the street to meet eyes with the little yellow dog I had seen before breakfast. My look may have let him know that I did not want to be friends. It wasn't that I didn't like dogs, but I had decided cats were my favorite. I couldn't turn my heart away from Amber. Seeing the little dog reminded me how I missed Amber so and how she waked me with soft purrs in the mornings.

Papa set up all the pieces he had created before we began our journey. He must have had more than two dozen. Then he began to create some new ones while we sat. As he carved, I decided to take out my journal and write a few words about Little Green and what it was like to me. Then I made a few sketches of the quaint street-scape to remember something of how it looked. Alongside the red wooden bench that sat nicely in the front of the bakery across from where I sat, was the little yellow dog. My hand and my pencil decided to include him in my sketch. I wondered if the baker shared any delicacies with him throughout the day. He looked patient enough to wait for them.

Papa continued to work, only looking up when required of him. I thought that made it more appealing for the town's people to approach him. "Beautiful, beautiful red bird," said a tiny lady who must have been as old as Papa. Cheery and spry, her age had not slowed her steps or her spirit. Papa slowly looked up from his work and grinned when he greeted the pretty lady. I wondered if she reminded him of Pippa Pearl and if Papa would ever love or marry again. They shared small talk for a few minutes, and the lady purchased the red bird to brighten her home. I imagined that she might have been a widower. After her visit, Papa seemed a little more alive.

Papa sold quite a few pieces that day and planned on staying on for the next. Willie and I were playing cards on the wooden porch of the store when a few other children about Willie's age arrived. They looked on as hand after hand I began to defeat Willie. Over the next few minutes, I had easily overthrown him. The children squealed in excitement. Willie had never been beaten in cards, and they knew he had received his due.

I looked up and met eyes with several boys and girls. Each one was as curious as the next. Willie silently stepped inside and grabbed a leather ball, as if it was the routine on Saturdays. Everyone began to play.

Soon, more children arrived to join in the game, and more folks stopped by to visit with Papa and shop his and the store's wares.

The yellow dog crossed the street filled with children to sit and watch from the porch of the store. There was something about his eyes that intrigued me. They were deep, dark and kind — a nice contrast with his yellow coat. The dog appeared to call the town streets his home but was not extremely poor in size. Mr. Wilson came out with some meat scraps to feed him, which answered my questions as to why.

"What's the dog's name," I called out from our game. "Oh, we just call him, that dog. He's a pretty good little dog mostly. He comes around once and a while for some scraps. We haven't really taken the time to give him a proper name. Why don't you, Willie and the children come up with one."

"That's a grand idea," I shouted. As the ball flew swiftly past my head, I screamed "stop." "Let's give this little fellow a proper name." "I will." "Let me." They all chimed in for an opportunity. "Let's each come up with a name and then we'll let the dog chose." The idea sounded reasonable to me, and evidently to the children.

After several minutes, every child's head began to nod in acknowledgment that a name had been selected. "Everyone, make a line, side by side. Each one of us will have a chance to call out our name and the one the dog likes best, will be the winner." Everyone agreed and took their places in line.

The little yellow dog sat across from our makeshift line on the front steps of the General Store. Ears alert, as if he was ready to be entertained. A small crowd began to form around our group. Then one by one the names were called.

"Max"

"Leonardo"

"Jessie"

"Rufus"

"Billie"

"Scruffy"

"Fido"

The dog looked on but didn't budge. I looked at the curious creature and thought for a moment before hollering out in my best dog call, "Scamp."

We all chuckled deeply as he started wagging his tail vigorously and making his way towards me in a galloping cantor. "Scamp, Scamp, we all laughed as we called out. Your name is Scamp little fellow." He barked as if to howl at the same time, taking on an almost welcome home glow.

The children and I sat down with little Scamp and talked about names for a bit, and how being named was part of being loved. It meant you belonged to someone. It meant that someone loved you enough to give you an identity, an identity that was all yours. They were excited for Scamp, and that he had a new name — one that he liked.

"How did you think of Scamp, Ms. Gracie," asked Peter a little toe-headed boy. "I don't think I did, Peter; It's no name I have ever thought of or favored. I think Scamp thought of it, or just knew it in his heart. So Scamp it is!"

"Ms. Gracie, this means something," said Willie excitedly. "It means Scamp is your dog, well, since you named him and all." I laughed. I had never thought of having a dog. I had never thought of it at all. Speechless I grinned and shook my head no, and as I looked up, I saw Papa sitting at the table with a smirk and a wink nodding affirmatively.

Summer travels with Papa had come to an end. The journey home felt satisfying. The wagon seemed fuller with Scamp and a journal full of ideas and sketches, while Papa's heart and mine seemed to have grown too. The people were wonderful and friendly everywhere we stopped, almost like family or old friends. They were truly a breath of fresh air.

When we arrived home to the farm, it felt as if things had changed. I was more fond of "home" now than ever. Perhaps, leaving for a while made me appreciate the quaintness of it all. "Absence does make the heart grow fonder," I thought.

Mama heard our arrival and stepped outside to greet us. Following her were curious little girls peeping on. My heart jumped when I saw them all standing there. I had missed them all so much, and I knew they would be ecstatic over Scamp. "No time to plan surprises, what will be, will be," I hurriedly concluded in my mind.

Mama was in her blue dress with her hair all swept up. I had forgotten how truly beautiful she was. She smiled as her hands clasped together over her heart and our wagon came to a halt. As we moved out of the wagon, all three of us. I'm not sure what happened. Mama laughed, cried, hollered and smiled all simultaneously. The girls screamed and started chasing Scamp around the trees. I glanced at Papa, standing there proudly. He was more handsome than ever. It felt like we were truly home. Almost like leaving was part of finding home and Scamp was meant to be part of it.

Daddy had traveled into town to take care of some business with Mr. Jake and returned by supper time. It was good

to be home. Papa stayed on for supper, and we shared stories
of our travels.

After supper, Daddy told us about a little boy that had lost
his parents. His father died in war and his mother to sickness.
The boy's mother was a family friend to Daddy when he was
growing up, close to him like a cousin, but not blood kin.
They didn't have any other relatives to take the little boy in,
so he was going to be sent to the orphanage in a neighboring
town. Daddy shared about how his Grandfather Emerson,
who died when I was a very small child, had been orphaned
too. The kind people that took him in became part of our
family. Part of our story. I could see it in Daddy's eyes that he
wanted to help. "What's his name Daddy?" little Eliza asked.
"His name is Daniel, and he is eight years old."

"I wonder if he knows much about the farm life?" Mama
inquired. "Yes, and I wonder if he can play checkers?" said
Ginny. "Bet I'll beat him good!" Everybody laughed. Even
Scamp seemed to have a smile on his face.

Family life seemed back to usual as Daniel moved his
way right into our home and into our hearts. His curious
ways were entertaining, and his smile was contagious. Ginny
was right, she did beat him good at checkers, but it wasn't
long before Daniel gave her a nice run for her money.

Mama and Daddy were supportive of my new friendship
with Paul and seemed somewhat fond of him. They knew not
to push about our relationship—so they did not.

There was something about Paul. His eyes, his smile —
his heart. I wasn't sure if we were friends or something more,

but somehow the thought of questioning it never crossed my
mind. In his presence, all seemed well and good enough. His
eyes sparkled onto mine with each glance, as if to share in the
light of the moment. The long pauses in conversation did not
seem awkward, yet refreshing. When I would sit with Paul
and talk about things, like what life was like in Ireland, his
beautiful way with words made normal conversations sound
like fascinating stories. Listening to him speak of everyday
life was like a poetic moment unfolding with each word and
each breath. The Irish accent only added more elegance and
mystery to his voice. Paul would tell me about Ireland, and
I would tell him stories of my life on the farm and of the
people in town. I began to realize how people and ways of
life had become one of my greatest interests.

I remembered the day I met him at the post office. I was
mailing off some letters to Willie and some others I had
met along my journey with Papa. I remember it well. I was
wearing a new dress that I had just put the finishing touches
on. The colors were all of the sea. There were blues of every
shade and a hint of green. It shimmered in the light of the
sun, as the fall skies were peaking. That day I felt beautiful.
There was something coming from the inside that I couldn't
describe. After I sent off my letters, I made my way towards
the door. As I approached it, it opened it from the other side.
He stood still with the door in one hand and his letter in the
other, as his eyes looked upon mine. I felt like I knew him,
but couldn't recall from when or where. After what felt like
a very long, but comfortable pause, he said in a soft but low
voice, "Gracie?" as if to question my existence. Surprised but
reassured, I grinned a bit and said "Yes?" in a questioning
tone of my own.

"I saw you that day, that day in the train depot, but you
didn't see me." My heart fluttered a bit. Could this be the
voice from the depot? The mysterious voice that had been

with me for all these months? "My name is Paul. Paul O'Brien," he rolled off his tongue with an Irish Brogue. His eyes twinkled as if to say nice to meet you, and I think mine twinkled back as if to say, "haven't I known you, forever?"

He stepped back and motioned me through the doorway and as I made my way across he said, "I know you're wondering who I am and how I know your name, Gracie." "Yes," was all I could say.

"You see, Walter Lee was my friend. He spoke of you on occasion. He loved you. He truly did. But there was something holding him back from loving you more. He felt sad about that." My eyes teared up as I nodded in agreement and Paul continued. "He described your beauty to me, and I could picture you in my mind. Your face I would never forget. I wasn't sure why, but I knew I would never forget it," Paul whispered.

Paul took my hand and held it between his as our eyes met for the last time that day. Tears filled my eyes as I looked into his as if to say goodbye, but I'll see you again soon.

As I walked away, I thought about Walter and why he couldn't love me, and how he had to die, and how Paul had come, and so many things went swirling through my mind.

Paul became very quiet as we sat across from one another. I moved my eyes to the floor as to not rush his thoughts. It was then that I noticed my oxblood colored boots could use a little shining. Even still, I loved the way they looked.

After several moments of silence, It was "Stella." The word Stella came out of Paul's mouth. He spoke it like it was an epiphany of sorts. "Yes, Paul?" I inquired. The word Stella sounded so beautiful to me. Paul replied, "Stella could be the name of the play. It's an Irish name, that means star. I heard it as a young boy, and it was so significant to me for some reason." My heart embraced the name, the word Stella, as if not to question it. "Stella," I said, as my mouth formed into a grin I could no longer hide. "Stella," Paul said as his voice raised into almost a shout and he stood to hug me. Stella may have been the most beautiful word we had ever heard.

We started making notes about who Stella was. A young, poor farm girl. In Ireland. Beautiful. Kind. What is her dilemma? Does she become ill? Is she very poor? Is she orphaned? Oh, and that voice. That beautiful voice of Stella.

As Stella's story developed into something deeper and deeper, and her character started to emerge, I sometimes wondered if Stella would be the one, the who would help Olivia and I mend bridges, and in a larger way bring our community closer together.

Word began to spread through town of Stella's arrival. One person to the other, one by one, the thought of Stella seemed to bring a sparkle of hope to our town. Paul and I would meet almost daily to work. I was boarding above the General Store in town during the week, and Daddy would take me back home for Sunday Church and to spend time with family each weekend.

We would begin each morning with a cup of coffee and breakfast before we started writing the next story of Stella. Usually, we worked in the General Store, the cafe or sometimes we would go into the playhouse to get a feel for the stage and how the stories would play out. Often times, some of the teenagers and children in town would accompany us and just sit on quietly and listen.

Paul would leap onto the stage and begin reciting the character lines. Being on stage seemed to help him polish out the rough spots for the parts. Sometimes I would join him.

In the evenings I would help Mrs. Wilson clean the dishes and sweep up the store. Sometimes I hand washed laundry and linens for her. The evening chores were to cover my room and board while I stayed in town to work on the play. I was pleased that Mama and Daddy were supportive of the idea. I had never done anything like it before and all in all, it seemed a little far fetched, but they believed in me enough to give it a chance.

Finally, the day came when all the lines were written, and all the scenes were portrayed. The beautiful Stella had come to life in our hearts and changed us in so many ways. It would be so difficult to describe what an effect she had on Paul and me.

We found a young artist to draw a design for our casting call posters. Guiding him in the image of Stella, he took our cues and began to bring to life a Stella, more real and more beautiful than even we had conjured.

"Smallish frame like a dancers figure; light brown wavy hair falling just below her shoulders, but swept up most of the time; iridescent eyes in earthy tones, with a quality of sadness conflicting with hope; naturally red lips; feminine and weak, yet strong in some ways; a dusty rose, beige dress with tattered edges and bare feet was how we imagined her.

"Auditions for the play September 26th. Come one. Come all."

"Why, Mr. Greely, fancy seeing you here," I said in surprise as we opened the doors for the auditions, and there he was at the head of the line. There was something different about Mr. Greely that day. He looked hopeful and healthy, and as far as I could tell – sober. I knew we could be taking our chances on him not staying that way, but for Mr. Greely, we would.

Paul chimed in "So, Mr. Greely is it?" "Yes, James Greely, and you?" "I'm Paul O'Brien. Nice to make your acquaintance." "And yours," he replied with a smile hiding under anticipation. I realized then that Paul and Mr. Greely had never met and that I would not need to tell Paul about Mr. Greely's struggles with alcohol, and how the town had shunned him in so many ways. Paul's eyes looked so understanding and accepting on Mr. Greely, so much so, that I wondered if his heart might have detected something deeper than what was on the surface. That was the thing about Paul, his heart and those eyes — those beautiful affirming eyes.

I wasn't sure how we would cast the parts or conduct the auditions, knowing that the people were unfamiliar with the characters or what role they might like to play. However, it didn't take long for me to notice that Paul had a plan. He didn't ask too many questions. But he did ask of Mr. Greely, "So James, what inspired you to come here today?" James looked down for a moment as if he was deciding whether to make up an answer or just tell us the truth. Then his eyes rose back up to ours as he said, " Hope. It was hope that brought me here today. Life has a way of repeating itself you know. We become something of the same, be it good or bad if we have no hope for anything different. I feel inspired to be a part of that change and that message. In fact, I believe I have been waiting to do something like this all my life." Mr. Greely had an interesting voice. It was vibrant and rich with just the right amount of depth to carry to an audience.

Paul shuffled hurriedly through some papers until he came to the one with the opening lines for the narrator. He turned his head my way as I looked at the paper to give a confirming glance. I nodded almost invisibly just before Paul handed the paper to Mr. Greely and gestured his hand towards the stage for Mr. James Greely to step up. He began by clearing his throat just a touch, before launching in so beautifully.

"The days seemed longer than usual as the spring light began to paint itself more abundantly across the blues of the Irish sky. The landscape united all aglow with the smiling faces of dandelions and poppies welcoming in a new season. From a bird's eye view, the village appeared to be making preparations for something or someone. Something or someone they had been waiting on for as long as they could remember."

Astonished by his presentation, Paul and I could not have imagined it any more beautiful. Mr. Greely was a natural at narrating. As I looked back to the door, I saw Celeste, Mr. Jenkins, Molly Wilson and Eliza at the head of the line. Peeking around from behind was my new little brother Daniel. I smiled to myself as I imagined the possibilities. "Stella" was coming to life.

ABOUT THE AUTHOR

Anne Tripp Wyatt is an emerging short story author, avid up-cycler, wife, and mother of two daughters. She enjoys playing and listening to music and spending time in nature with her family. Nostalgic ways and ideas have always been interesting to me," she says. Growing up on the family's 'Century Farm' where traditions have been passed down for over 100 years, Anne Tripp Wyatt considers herself a modern woman, steeped in the ways of "old." Recounting stories of a life long ago from both sides of her family, Anne Tripp Wyatt has a collection of thoughts and ideas from the past that have inspired a series of fiction short stories. She craves the simple life and tries to embody those lost philosophies in her stories and in her day to day life. She and her family currently reside in Travelers Rest, South Carolina.

Gracie Emerson